Summer Rain

OTHER WORKS BY MARGUERITE DURAS

Emily L.
India Song
L'Amante Anglaise
Blue Eyes, Black Hair
Four Novels: The Afternoon of Mr. Andesmas;
  Ten-Thirty on a Summer Night;
  Moderato Cantabile; The Square
The Malady of Death
Hiroshima Mon Amour
The Vice-Consul
Destroy, She Said
Outside: Selected Writings
The Ravishing of Lol Stein
The Sailor from Gibraltar
The War: A Memoir
The Lover

Summer Rain

Marguerite Duras

Translated from the French
by Barbara Bray

Charles Scribner's Sons

NEW YORK

MAXWELL MACMILLAN CANADA

TORONTO

MAXWELL MACMILLAN INTERNATIONAL

NEW YORK   OXFORD   SINGAPORE   SYDNEY

Charles Scribner's Sons   Maxwell Macmillan Canada, Inc.
Macmillan Publishing Company   1200 Eglinton Avenue East
866 Third Avenue   Suite 200
New York, NY 10022   Don Mills, Ontario M3C 3N1

Macmillan Publishing Company is part of the Maxwell Communication Group of Companies.

Library of Congress Cataloging-in-Publication Data
Duras, Marguerite.
     [Pluie d'été. English]
     Summer rain / Marguerite Duras; translated from the French
by Barbara Bray.
          p.   cm.
     Translation of: La pluie d'été.
     ISBN 0-684-19403-1
     I. Title.
     PQ2607.U8245P5813   1992   91-37345   CIP
843'.912—dc20

Originally published as *La pluie d'été* by P.O.L, Paris, in 1990.

Design by Ellen R. Sasahara

10 9 8 7 6 5 4 3 2 1

Printed in the United States of America

For Hervé Sors

Summer Rain

Books, the father used to find them on suburban trains. Or piled up separately, as if they were being given away as presents, beside garbage bins after someone had died or moved out. Once he found *The Life of Georges Pompidou.* He read that twice. There were bundles of old technical magazines as well, left beside ordinary garbage bins, but he didn't bother with those. The mother read *The Life of Georges Pompidou* too. They were both fascinated. Afterward they looked for other *Lives of the Famous*—there were various series called that—but they never found another one that interested them as much as the life of Georges Pompidou, perhaps because they didn't know the other people's names. They stole the books from the second-hand boxes outside bookstores. The *Lives* were so cheap the store owners didn't do anything about it.

The father and mother liked the story of Georges Pompidou's life better than any novel. It wasn't just because he was famous that they were interested in him, but because, although he was so distinguished, the authors of the book had written his life in terms of the pattern common to all lives. The father saw something of himself in the life of Georges Pompidou, the mother saw something of herself in that of his wife. Those other two lives were not alien to them; they even had some parallels with their own.

Except as regards the children, said the mother.

True, said the father. Except as regards the children.

It was the way the people in the biographies lived their everyday lives that interested them, not the unusual facts or events that made each one's fate peculiarly fortunate or tragic. Though, to tell the truth, even these unusual destinies did sometimes resemble one another. But until they read the Pompidou book the father and mother didn't know how much their own lives resembled other people's.

All lives were the same, the mother said, except as regards the children. You couldn't tell about the children.

No, said the father. You couldn't tell about the children.

Once they'd started a book the parents always finished it, even if it soon turned out to be boring and took months to get through. This was the case with Edouard Herriot's *Forêt Normande*, which didn't have any people in it and was only about the Normandy forest from beginning to end.

The parents were foreigners who'd come to Vitry about twenty years before, perhaps more than twenty years before. They'd met and got married there. Allowed to stay on through a series of residence permits, one after another, they were still there on only a temporary basis. Even though they'd been there such a long time. They were unemployed. No one would ever give them a job because they didn't know much about their origins and they had no training or skills. They themselves never pressed the point. Their children were born in Vitry too, including the eldest, who died. It was because of the children that they were given somewhere to live. When the second child was born, the local authorities said they could occupy a house scheduled for demolition until a unit became available in a public housing project. But the public housing project was never built, and they went on living in the two-room house—a kitchen and a bedroom—until, seeing another child arrive every year, the local authorities had a flimsy annex built on, consisting of a kind of dormitory separated from the kitchen by a corridor. Jeanne and Ernesto, the eldest of the seven children, slept in the corridor. The other five slept in the dormitory. The Catholic Aid Society donated some oil-fired stoves still in good condition.

The question of the children's education never seriously bothered the City Hall, the children, or the parents. The parents did once ask for a teacher to be sent to give the children lessons, but the authorities said what a nerve, whatever next? That's how it always was. All the official reports about them pointed out how uncooperative they were, and the extraordinary way they persisted in being difficult.

And so they read books they found on trains or outside second-hand bookstores or beside garbage bins. They did ask to be allowed to use the Vitry public library. But the authorities said that beat all, so the parents let it drop. Luckily there were still the suburban trains for finding books, and the garbage bins. The father and mother had free passes on public transportation because of all the children they had, and they often made the journey to Paris and back. Especially after they'd read the book about Georges Pompidou, which absorbed them for a whole year.

Once there was another book incident in the family. It concerned the children, and happened in early spring.

At that time Ernesto must have been between twelve and twenty years old. Just as he didn't know how to read, so he didn't know his own age. All he knew was his name.

It happened in the space under the ground floor of a nearby house, a kind of shed that the people who lived there always left open for the children, who used to go and wait there until dinner time every evening after it got dark, or in the afternoon if the weather was cold or wet. It was here, by the central heating pipes, under some rubble, that the smallest of the brothers* found the book. They took it to Ernesto, who looked at it for a long time. It was a very thick book bound in black leather, and a hole had been burned right through it by what must have been some terribly powerful implement like a blowtorch or a red-hot iron bar. The hole was perfectly circular, and around it the rest of the book was unscathed, so it must have been possible to read what remained of each page. The children had seen other books in bookstore windows and in their parents' house, but they'd never seen one so cruelly treated before. The youngest brothers and sisters cried.

In the days that followed this discovery, Ernesto entered into a period of silence. He would stay in the shed all afternoon, cooped up alone with the burned book.

Then all of a sudden he must have remembered the tree.

There was a garden on the corner of the rue Berlioz and the nearly always deserted rue Camélinat, which led down a steep hill to the edge of the highway and the Port-à-l'Anglais. The garden was surrounded by a wire

---

*"Brothers" and "sisters" are in English throughout the original French text. *Tr.*

fence supported by iron posts, all very neat and tidy like the fences around all the other gardens in the street, which were about the same size and shape.

But this particular garden had no features. No flower-beds, no flowers, no plants, no bushes. Only a tree. Just one. The garden consisted simply of the tree.

The children had never seen any other trees like it. It was the only one in Vitry, perhaps in the whole of France. It might have seemed ordinary; you might not even have noticed it. But once you had noticed it you could never forget it. It was medium-sized. Its trunk was as straight as a line drawn on a blank page. Its dome-shaped foliage was thick and beautiful as a fine head of hair just emerging from the water. But underneath the mass of leaves the garden was a wilderness. There wasn't enough light for anything to grow there.

The tree was ageless, indifferent to season or latitude, irremediably alone. It was probably no longer mentioned in books about this country. Nor perhaps about any other.

Several days after the finding of the book, Ernesto went to see the tree, and he stayed near it, sitting on the bank opposite the fence that surrounded it. Then he started going there every day. Some days he stayed there a long time, but still always alone. He never said anything to anyone except Jeanne about his visits to the tree. Strangely enough, that was the only place where the brothers and sisters didn't come to look for him.

Perhaps it was the tree, on top of the burned book,

that started to drive him mad. That's what the brothers and sisters thought. But in what way mad—that they thought they'd never know.

One evening the brothers and sisters asked Jeanne what she thought; if she had any ideas about it. She thought Ernesto must have been struck by the loneliness both of the tree and of the book. She believed Ernesto must have seen the book, with the ordeal inflicted on it, and the tree, in its loneliness, as both suffering the same fate. Ernesto told her it was when he found the burned book that he remembered the imprisoned tree. He thought of both of them together, and of how to make their destinies touch, merge, and mingle in his, Ernesto's, own head and body, so that he might come to reach the unknown, the unknown of all life.

"And me too," she added. "Ernesto thought about me."

But the brothers and sisters didn't understand a word of what she said, and went to sleep. Jeanne didn't notice, and went on talking about the tree and Ernesto.

For Jeanne, after Ernesto spoke to her like that, the burned book and the tree became things belonging to Ernesto, things he had touched with his hands, his eyes, and his mind, and that he had given to her.

At that point in his life Ernesto was supposed not to be able to read, but he said he'd read some of the burned book. Just like that, he said, without thinking about it, without even knowing what he was doing. And then—

well, then he stopped bothering whether he was really reading or not, or even what reading was—whether it was this or something else. At first, he said, he'd tried like this: he took the shape of a word and quite arbitrarily gave it a provisional meaning. Then he gave the next word another meaning, but in terms of the assumed provisional meaning of the first word. And he went on like that until the whole sentence yielded some sense. In this way he came to see that reading was a kind of continuous unfolding within his own body of a story invented by himself. And thus it seemed to him the book was about a king who reigned in a country a long way away from France, a king who was a foreigner like himself, a very long time ago. He had the impression he'd been reading not many stories about many kings but the story of one king of a certain country at a certain time. Only part of his story, because of the way the book had been damaged—just some of the things he did and certain episodes in his life. He told his brothers and sisters about it. But they were jealous of the book, and said to him:

"How could you have read it, stupid, when you don't know how? Read? You? Since when?"

Ernesto agreed: he didn't know how he could have read the book without knowing how to read. He was rather puzzled about it himself. He told his brothers and sisters that too.

So then they all decided to check up on what he'd said. Ernesto went and saw a neighbor's son who *had* been to school, who still went, and who had a definite age: fourteen. Ernesto asked him to read the bit of the book *he* thought he'd read.

"What does it say, there at the front of the book?"

He also went to see a teacher in Vitry who had university degrees and who also had a definite age: thirty-eight.

And both of them said more or less the same thing: that it was a story about a king. A Jewish king, the teacher added. That was the only difference between the two interpretations. After this, Ernesto would have liked to check up with his father too, but strangely enough his father wriggled out of it, washed his hands of the problem, and told him he should believe what the teacher had said. Then the teacher came to see the parents and told them to send Ernesto to school, and his sister too. It wasn't right to keep children à la casa* when they were so intelligent and eager to learn.

"But what about the brothers and sisters?" asked Ernesto. "Who's going to look after them?"

"They can look after themselves," said the mother.

The mother agreed with the teacher, she said it was a good thing—now all the brothers and sisters would have to get used to Ernesto not being there. Some time or other they'd have to do without him, some time or other they'd all be separated for good. Meanwhile there were bound to be single separations. And later on whatever was left of it all would in due course evaporate too. That

---

*i.e., at home (a mixture of French and Italian). *Tr.*

was life. As for Ernesto, they'd forgotten to send him to school, it was easy to forget that sort of thing with him, but some time or other he too was bound to tear himself away from the brothers and sisters. That was life, that's all, just life. Leaving your parents, going to school—it was all the same.

So Ernesto went to Blaise Pascal, the grade school in Vitry-sur-Seine.

While he was at school his brothers and sisters waited every evening for him to come home, hiding on a patch of common land, once an alfalfa field and still covered with self-sown shoots, where people dumped their children's old toys, old scooters, old strollers, old tricycles, old bikes, and more old bikes. Whenever Ernesto came back from school or anywhere else, the brothers and sisters would follow him. Wherever he went, wherever he came back from, even later, even later still, when Ernesto had emerged from his period of silence, they kept on following him. When Ernesto went into the shed, they went too. There they would wait for the signal for dinner: a whistle from the father. And then they would go with Ernesto à la casa. The brothers and sisters never went into la casa without him.

Ernesto's incarceration in school lasted ten days. It passed entirely without incident.
For ten days Ernesto listened to the teacher carefully.

He didn't ask any questions.

And then, on the morning of the tenth day after he'd started school, Ernesto went back à la casa.

Early in the morning. In the kitchen, the main room in the house. A long rectangular table, some benches, and two chairs. This is where the mother usually is. She's the woman sitting watching Ernesto come in. She looks at him, then goes on peeling potatoes.

Atmosphere of gentleness.

Mother: Still a bit angry, aren't you, Ernestino.

Ernesto: Yes.

Mother: But why? . . . You don't know. As usual.

Silence.

Ernesto: That's right. I don't know.

The mother waits for a long while in silence for Ernesto to speak. She knows Ernesto well. He's angry inside. He looks outside, forgetting the mother. And then he comes back to her, and they look at each other. He says nothing. She lets him be. And then he speaks.

Ernesto: You're peeling potatoes.

Mother: Yes.

Silence. Then Ernesto shouts.

Ernesto: The world, there it is, all around us, with all sorts of things in it, every kind of event, and there you sit peeling potatoes from morn till night every day in the year . . . Couldn't you at least change to a different vegetable?

The mother. She looks at him.

Mother: Crying for a thing like that . . . are you crazy or something this morning?

Ernesto: No.

Gentleness is restored.

Long silence. The mother goes on peeling. Ernesto watches her.

Mother: Aren't you back from school a bit early, Ernestino?

The mother waits. Ernesto says nothing. Silence.

Mother: Perhaps you wanted to tell me something, Ernesto, eh?

Ernesto is slow to answer.

Ernesto: No. (Pause.) Yes.

Mother: It *can* happen . . . something to say . . .

Ernesto: It can.

Mother: But then I was thinking . . .

Ernesto: Yes.

Silence.

Mother: The opposite . . . that can happen too.

Ernesto: Yes.

Silence.

Mother: Please yourself, Ernesto.

Ernesto: Yes.

Silence.

Mother: Perhaps it's that what you want to tell me you can't tell me . . .

Ernesto: That's right. I can't . . .
The pace is slow, gentle.
Mother: Why not?
Ernesto: It would upset you, so I can't.
Mother: And why would it upset me?
Ernesto hesitates.
Ernesto: Because. And anyhow you wouldn't under-
stand what I said. And if you wouldn't understand it there
isn't any point in my saying it.
Mother: But if I didn't understand it it wouldn't up-
set me.
Ernesto is silent.
Mother: What are you going on about today, Vladi-
mir?
Ernesto: It's not what I'd say that would upset you.
You'd be upset because you wouldn't understand.
Silence. The mother looks at her son.
Mother: Tell me anyway, Vladimir . . . tell me *how* you'd
tell me if there *was* any point in your telling me . . .
Ernesto: Well . . . I'd be here just like now, watching
you peel potatoes, and then all of a sudden I'd tell
you, just like that. (Pause.) And then it would have been
said.
The mother waits. Silence.
Then Ernesto shouts.
Ernesto: Mama, I'd say . . . Mama, I'm not going back
to school because at school they teach me things I don't
know. Then it would have been said. Done. There you
are.

The mother stops peeling. Silence.

Mother, reciting, slowly: Because at school they teach me things I don't know . . .

Ernesto: Yeah.

The mother ponders. Then looks at Ernesto. Then smiles. Ernesto smiles too.

Mother: That's a good one.

Ernesto: Yeah.

Ernesto stands up, goes and gets a knife from a drawer, and comes back to the table.

Long look from the mother at her child Ernesto.

Silence.

Then all of a sudden they both laugh . . . Oh my. They laugh. They peel, they laugh.

Silence.

Ernesto: D'you understand what I told you, Mama?

Silence. The mother ponders.

Mother: Well . . . I couldn't say *how* I understand it . . . if I understand it right . . . but some of it, I think I do understand some of it, yes.

Ernesto: Leave it, Mama . . .

Mother: All right.

Silence.

The mother starts peeling again. Every so often she looks at her child, Ernesto.

Mother: Which number child are you, Vladimir?

Ernesto: Your first after the one that died. (Affectionately:) Every day you plague me with that question, Mama. Try and get it into your head once and for all.

I'm the first ... (Gesture:) 1 + 6 = 7 ... It's the same with that name you will call me by ... Vladimir ... Where did that come from? Mother Russia?

Silence. She doesn't answer.

Ernesto: So you did understand a bit what I was saying, Mama?

Mother: A bit ... but don't let's exaggerate ...

Ernesto: You're right. It doesn't do to exaggerate.

Silence. Then both of them are suddenly elated. Their love for each other suddenly explodes into delight.

Mother: The world's so backward ... Oh my, sometimes it all comes over you ...

Ernesto: Yes. But oh my, sometimes it isn't backward at all!

Mother, happy: That's right ... sometimes it's quite smart ... oh my ...

Ernesto: Yes! So smart ... it doesn't even realize ...

Silence. They go on peeling. They have calmed down.

Mother: Look, Ernestino, you'd better go find your brothers and sisters ... your father'll soon be home ... Maybe it'd be better if *I* told him what you've decided.

Ernesto: My father won't do anything to me ... he's a good guy ... incredibly good ...

Mother, doubtful: Good guy ... good guy ... Easily said. You'll see—he'll say: I understand, my boy ... He'll seem like that ... quite quiet, not looking for any trouble. And then all of a sudden he'll start picking on you ... enough to drive you crazy.

Silence.

Mother, gently: Go find your brothers and sisters, Ernesto ... go on. I know what I'm saying ...

Suddenly there's a flash of mistrust in Ernesto's expression.

Ernesto: Where *are* my brothers and sisters?

Mother: Where do you think? At the five-and-ten, of course ...

Ernesto, laughing: Sitting on the floor by the bookshelves ... reading coffee-table books.

Mother: Yeah. (She doesn't laugh.) Reading what? They don't know how. So? Reading what, I ask you? Ever since *you* read that book about the king, they keep going to the five-and-ten trying to read too ... But they're just pretending ... that's the truth of it.

Ernesto suddenly shouts.

Ernesto, shouting: Now they're supposed to be pretending, my brothers and sisters, are they? Never! Do you hear what I say, Mama? Those kids never pretend anything ... Never!

Mother, shouting too: That beats all! So what're they reading, eh? They *can't* read! So ... what *are* those kids reading?

Ernesto's shouts and his mother's—indistinguishable.

Ernesto, yelling: They're reading whatever they like, for godsake!

Mother, yelling too: But where, once and for all? Where *is* it, the writing they're supposed to be reading?

Ernesto: The writing's in the book, of course!

Mother: Next thing they'll be reading the stars!

They start laughing again, but this time it sounds hollow.

Ernesto, sober again: I don't like anyone to criticize my brothers and sisters. Sorry, Mama.

Ernesto gets up and goes.

The mother sits motionless. She has stopped peeling. She's pensive. But cheerful too. Intrigued.

The mother was just getting potatoes ready for her children. Fried with onions was how they liked them best. Every so often she'd make paprika stews that did for the whole week, almost. Other times she made rice puddings flavored with cinnamon, but they lasted only a couple of days. And other times still she made eel stew seasoned with herbs. She said she knew great marshlands by the river Scheldt where the fishermen lived on eel stew seasoned with herbs, and rice pudding flavored with cinnamon. As for paprika stew, she couldn't remember which country she'd got that from. The children listened, fascinated, to hear where the mother came from. What countries, what unknown things this mother of theirs had been through before she came here, to Vitry where her children awaited her. Never did they forget what the mother told them.

We're in the kitchen. Three days have gone by since Ernesto's announcement. The mother hasn't told anyone. She's there, alone, sitting at the table. In front of her are the potatoes. She has a knife in her hand. But she's not peeling the potatoes. She's looking out at the yard, away toward the river and the new town. She's beautiful, the mother. Reddish blond hair. Big green eyes. Jeanne has her mother's eyes, and her hair. But she's not so tall. The mother is often silent. She just looks. When she walks, something in her body suggests an inner fatigue, the result of her many pregnancies. Her breasts are probably heavier than they should be, less taut than they must have been when she was young. You can see this although she's still beautiful: she hasn't done anything to counter the effects of the weariness caused by the childbearing Emilio imposes on her every year. Today she's wearing a dark red dress that came from the City Hall. Sometimes the social services there give her dresses, and these are occasionally very pretty, often almost new. They also provide a lot of things for the children, a lot of sweaters and tee-shirts. The mother doesn't have any worries on that score, except for Emilio. The City Hall won't provide anything for the father because they say he doesn't deserve it. Sometimes the mother wears her hair loose, that's how she's got it today, her hair's down to her shoulders, reddish blond against the dark red of the dress. The mother has forgotten the language of her youth. She speaks like all the other people in Vitry, and without an accent. She only makes mistakes in the conjugations of the verbs. But there survive from her past certain ineffaceable sounds, soft words that she seems to be paying out slowly, chanting sounds that moisten the inside of her voice and sometimes make the words emerge from her body without her realizing it, as if she were being visited by the memory of a language long forsaken.

Enter Emilio. She hasn't heard him come in. She has been preoccupied, the mother has, these last few days.

Father: Well, are you peeling the potatoes or aren't you?

Mother: I'm peeling them.

Father: Doesn't look like it to me.

Silence.

Father: What is it? Why are you acting this way?

Mother: It's Ernesto. He doesn't want to go back to school. He says once is enough.

Silence.

Father, muttering: Well I'm blowed! (Silence.) Mind you, I understand the boy ... I can see his point of view ...

Mother: No.

Father: Yes, I can. What I don't see is why he had to say it. If you ask me he should have just kept quiet. All he had to do was simply not go. Why did he have to make a song about it?

Mother: Why not? It's nothing disgraceful.

Silence.

Father: How did he say it? Let's hear.

Silence.

Mother: He said: I'm never going back to school again because . . .

Father: Because what?

Mother: Because.

Father: Because nothing?

The mother shouts.

Mother: Yeah, that's right!

The father restrains himself.

Father: Watch out, Natasha . . . I'm going to lose my temper in a minute . . .

Mother: I'm trying to think.

It slowly comes back to her.

Mother: He said . . . because at school . . . they teach me things I know . . . There . . . that's more or less it.

The father ponders.

Father: It can't be . . . you must have misunderstood . . . That's crazy . . . He can't have said that.

Mother: And why not?

Father: Because he doesn't know anything.

Mother: So what?

Father: He can't complain about being taught what he knows because he doesn't know anything. Ernesto can't have said that.

The mother remembers.

Mother: It must be the opposite . . . Yes . . . it's the opposite.

Father: The opposite of what?

22

Mother: Just a minute . . .

Silence. The mother tries to remember again, and succeeds.

Mother: He said: I'll never go back to school again because they teach me things I don't know. There, that's it . . .

Father: I see . . . That's more like it . . . That's a bit more like my boy.

The father hasn't understood. The mother suspects as much.

Mother: Are you sure, Emilio?

Father: No . . . but . . .

Mother: You've never had much . . . affinity with Ernesto, Emilio.

Father: Yes, I have . . . He doesn't know it, but . . .

Silence.

Father: What do *you* think?

Mother: I don't think there's anything to understand about it directly. But at the same time it's very odd, Emilio . . . Ever since Ernesto said what he did, it's as if I kept hearing it all the time . . . As if, if you really wanted it to mean something . . . well, in the end it would mean something . . .

Father: Mean mischief, you mean . . .

Mother: Not necessarily . . . not necessarily, Emilio.

Father: It's since he said that that you think this—is that what you mean, Natasha?

Mother: Since then. Yes.

Silence.

Father: So that was what he was cooking up, your precious Ernesto. He's so different from the others it was bound to come out in the end.

The mother is horrified by the words her husband has just used.

Mother: Different from the others ... I don't see it ...

Father: What do you mean, you don't see it?

Mother: They all seem the same to me. Perhaps it's the maternal instinct ...

Father: Yes.

Silence.

Father: So you say you didn't notice Ernesto was different from the others?

Mother: I wouldn't go so far as that ... But I don't agree ... It's the opposite, more like ... You *could* say he's too much *like* the others ...

Father: So you don't understand?

Mother: It might be he eats a bit less than the others, is that it? Perhaps it's to do with his size? If it's not that, what *is* it? You've seen him, you know how tremendous he is! No one would believe he's twelve years old. And grave as a bishop, too.

Father: Try to think, Natasha ... Haven't you noticed anything else? Anything at all?

Mother: Now I come to think of it ... yes ... He doesn't say anything. That's it ...

Father: That's it ... And when he does say something, this is what happens. He doesn't just say pass me the salt. He says things no one's ever said before. Things that take some thinking of. Things not every Tom, Dick, or Harry could dream up . . .

Ernesto's brothers and sisters were all like Ernesto. Like the mother and like Ernesto. They'd been like the father when they were very small. Then for two or three years they weren't like anything. Then all of a sudden they were like the mother and Ernesto. But there was one who was still not like anyone, and that was Jeanne. She was between eleven and seventeen years old. The mother said if there was one of them who was beautiful and indifferent to her own beauty it was her, Jeanne.

The mother thought what Jeanne took for her belief in God had something to do with her feeling for her brother Ernesto. The mother was pleased rather than otherwise that this should be so. Nothing wrong or bad could come from that aspect of her life. And so the mother was blind about herself: she didn't see that she herself was made in the image of those two children of hers.

When Jeanne was small she was so fond of looking at fire, so fascinated by it, that the mother took her to the local clinic. They analyzed her blood. It was in her blood that they saw Jeanne was an arsonist. But apart from her slightly extravagant love of fire she was a very fine girl, strong and everything, Just look at her, the mother told the brothers and sisters, she said all they had to do was not leave her alone with fire, because she didn't realize she had this extravagance any more than she knew about her own beauty, her own laughter. So she might forget, lose her wits by looking at fire too much, and even, so the clinic had told her, actually start conflagrations in her own home. That was all, the mother told them. The brothers and sisters were at once amazed and frightened at the thought that their adored sister was so strongly attracted by a thing like fire. Jeanne herself blushed with pleasure at being the object of so much interest on the part of her brothers and sisters.

The mother feared both the little girl's love for Ernesto and her love of fire. In the mother's eyes, Jeanne lived in a region of danger unknown to everyone, including the mother, who had a feeling she herself never would approach it. But was it really unknown to her? she wondered. Was she sure? Yes, the mother was sure she never would approach it, that silent region, that kind of intelligence that inhabited Jeanne and Ernesto.

It was Jeanne who asked Ernesto to tell how he had left school, to say what had happened. She herself had been going to school for three days without seeing very clearly what she could do there except, one day, leave.

She told Ernesto she thought he ought to talk to the whole family, to the smallest brothers and sisters as well as their giant of a mother, about how he'd left school.

Several times Ernesto refused. Then Jeanne implored him. And once she kissed him, weeping, and said he didn't love them any more. For the first time Ernesto felt Jeanne's face against his own. Smelled her ocean smell, floral, salty.

Ernesto's arms closed around Jeanne's body. The two of them stood there like that, silent, eyes lowered, hidden from themselves like lovers the next morning.

There was a long pause, during which they were pervaded by a silent knowledge impossible ever to forget.

They parted without looking at each another.

Jeanne didn't ask Ernesto again to tell the family about his leaving school.

And yet it was on the evening of that same day, after dinner, that Ernesto told the story of how one leaves school.

Ernesto is standing by the front steps, in the light shade of the cherry tree. The mother is in her usual place.

Emilio sits facing her. Behind Ernesto is Jeanne, lying on the ground behind her brother, facing the wall.

Ernesto tells how it was, how he left school, how it happened—apparently without his really intending it.

Ernesto speaks very slowly, what he says seems quite clear. It's as if he were talking to someone not there, or else someone hard of hearing. Perhaps he's really talking to her, talking for the benefit of the younger sister lying by the wall apparently asleep.

That day, says Ernesto, I waited all morning in the classroom.
I didn't know why.

Once it was break.
It seemed very far away.

I found myself alone.

I could hear shouts, all the usual noises of break.
I think I was afraid.
I don't know what of.

And then it was over.

I went on waiting.
I had to go on waiting, I didn't know why.

Another time it was the cafeteria.
I could hear the sound of plates and voices.
It was pleasant. I forgot I had to run away.

It was after the cafeteria that it happened. Suddenly I
couldn't hear anything any more.

That was when it happened.
I stood up.
I was afraid I wouldn't make it. Wouldn't manage to
stand up and then get away.

But I did make it.

I walked out of the classroom.

In the schoolyard I saw the others coming back from
the cafeteria.

I walked very slowly.

And then I found myself outside the school.
On a road.

The fear had gone.
I wasn't afraid any more.

I sat down under the trees by the water tower.

And I waited. I don't know if I waited a long time or not very long.

I think I went to sleep.

Silence. Ernesto shuts his eyes and remembers.

It's as if it were a thousand years ago.

Silence.
It looks as if Ernesto has forgotten.
And then he remembers.

Ernesto: I understood something I still find it hard to express ... I'm still too small to say it properly. Something like the creation of the universe. I was rooted to the spot: all of a sudden I was looking at the creation of the universe ...
Silence.
Father: Ernesto, you wouldn't be going a little far, would you ...
Silence.
Mother: And have you anything to say about it, Ernesto?
Ernesto: Not much.

Silence.

Ernesto: Listen ... it must have happened all at once. In one night. By the morning everything was set. All the forests, the mountains, the baby rabbits, everything. Just one night. It created itself. In just one night. Everything was there. All as it should be. Except for one thing. Just one.

Mother: If it was missing from the start, that thing, how can we tell it was missing at all?

Ernesto is silent. Then he goes on.

Ernesto: It wasn't something you saw. It was something you knew.

Silence.

Ernesto: It's something ... you think you ought to be able to say what it was ... but at the same time you know it's impossible to express ... It's personal ... You think you could ... should be able to ... but no ...

The mother is suddenly gleeful. She laughs.

Mother: *I* know what was missing: the wind!

Father: No, that was there too. The wind was there right away. Don't you start, Ginetta!

Ernesto: Well, actually ... It's almost impossible to say exactly: everything was there and yet there was no point. No point. No point at all.

Silence.

Father: The little things, they were there too ...

Ernesto: Yes. The very smallest things, and all the little invisible things, the little particles—they were all there.

Not one little pebble missing, not one little child, and yet there was no point. Not a leaf of a tree missing. And there was no point.

Silence.

Father: You say: there was no point.

Ernesto: No point.

Mother: I could listen to it for hours, what you say.

Silence.

Ernesto: Continents, governments, oceans, rivers, elephants, ships—no point.

Sister: Music.

Ernesto pauses slightly before replying.

Ernesto: No point.

Father: What's it mean, there was no point? I don't quite follow. Explain.

Ernesto: You can't explain it. There's no point in saying it, either.

Mother: School? No point in school either?

Ernesto: No point. You know that better than anyone.

Silence.

Ernesto: Who would it have had any point for—life? Or school? Who for? What for? So there's no point in the rest.

Silence. The mother gets angry.

Mother: Who *said* there wasn't any point?

Ernesto: No one.

Mother: Oh dear, whatever next, whatever next!

Father: You're not starting again, are you, Natasha?

Mother: They're connected, then, school and the universe?

Ernesto: Very closely.

Mother: Funny—I'm beginning to understand . . .

Ernesto: You never stopped understanding, you're the most brilliant person in the universe . . .

Father: All the same, Ernesto . . . All the same . . .

Mother: Yes . . . All the same . . . Your father's right.

Father: The teacher, you have to go see him anyway.

Ernesto, not answering: Dear parents . . .

Mother: That sounds funny in this house—"Dear parents . . ."

Father: Yes, it does.

Smiles. They feel happy.

Mother, very politely: All the same. I don't want to go to prison.

The father, suddenly galvanized, shouts.

Father, to Ernesto: How often do you have to be told? They punish people for skipping school. It starts with the parents, they go to prison, and it ends up with the child, he goes to prison too. So they all wind up in prison. And if there's a war on, they're executed. So there!

Now Ernesto starts to giggle quietly.

Mother: You're going against the law, Ernesto . . . what you're saying, it's not on . . .

Ernesto: All you have to do is say I've got flu, that I keep getting chicken pox or scarlet fever or whatever . . .

Mother: He doesn't believe in physical illnesses, the teacher . . . Oh my . . . and anyhow the time for that sort of illness ended a long time ago . . .

Father: And anyhow it's beginning to get around . . . what you said . . . It's all over the neighborhood already. Everyone thinks it's a great joke, but it's not very nice for us . . .

Ernesto laughs. Then silence.

Ernesto, very gently: I must go and pick up my brothers and sisters from the five-and-ten.

Mother: They'll be reading books now about the world going up in smoke, won't they? Oh my . . .

She laughs at the thought of the children reading such things.

Ernesto laughs too. So does Jeanne.

Ernesto: Explosions, bombings, and so on. Oh my . . . That's how it is . . . I read that stuff myself sometimes. Oh my! There are the kids, sitting on the floor by the shelves, good as gold . . . The shop assistants actually give them coffee-table books to look at, they're so good . . .

The parents laugh.

Ernesto: We're so well brought up we sit and read. The last book was *Tintin at the Five-and-Ten.* It was all about Tintin reading. Reading where? At the five-and-ten!

Everyone laughs.

Mother: Well, I must say . . . these writers don't exhaust themselves looking for subjects . . .

But now the father is galvanized again and shouts.

Father: Anyhow, there's no getting away from it, we'll have to see the teacher and explain. We can't go trying old tricks like flu and chicken pox and such. We must tell the truth. Inform the teacher that our son Ernesto doesn't wish to go to school any more.

Mother: And what will your famous teacher's answer be? A few kicks up the backside, I imagine!

Father: Not necessarily . . . He *might* say he understands Ernesto's decision and will bear it in mind. Anyhow, we have to go and see him. They bug *us* to send the children to school, so we have to bug *them* when they don't go. It's only polite.

The white town descended the slopes in stages to the dreadful highway that ran along by the river. Between the highway and the river lay Vitry New Town, which had nothing in common with our Vitry. Our Vitry consisted of little houses. And the New Town was all apartment blocks. But what the children knew first and foremost was that below their own town was the highway and the trains. And that after the trains came the river. The trains went along by the river and the highway went along by the railway line. And so if there was a flood the highway would become another river.

The trains, said Ernesto, went by at four hundred kilometers an hour. What with that and the echo from the highway, the noise was terrible, your heart was crushed by it, and your head couldn't think.

It was true. It was as if the highway were the bed of the river. The river was the Seine. The highway was lower than the Seine. So the children's dream of seeing the highway flooded, even once, was not too farfetched. But it had never happened.

It was made of concrete, the highway, and by now the concrete was covered with black moss. It had cracked in lots of places, making deep holes, and in the holes grass and other plants still sprouted with revolting determination. But after twenty years they'd become concrete grass and plants, black and oozing.

It was at once true and untrue that the highway was disused, for cars did go by every so often. Sometimes it was new cars whizzing along through the wind. Sometimes it was old trucks racketing peacefully past, so used to it all that their drivers dozed off.

Every day the children of the family we're talking about were out and about. Looking at things. Walking around. Rushing through the streets, along the roads, the paths on the hillside, the shopping mall, the parks, the empty houses. They ran a lot. Of course the small ones couldn't run as fast as the big ones. And the big ones were always afraid of losing them. So they would start off alongside them and then double back and come up behind them. So then the little ones thought they'd got ahead of the older ones and were very pleased with themselves.

The little brothers and sisters had always been the bane of Ernesto's and Jeanne's existence, but Ernesto and Jeanne didn't know it. Whenever the brothers and sisters lost sight of the two older ones they were seized with terror. They couldn't see them walk away or disappear around a street corner without screaming with terror, as if only they, the younger ones, still knew what it would be like if ever they lost their elder brother and sister, and the older ones themselves had forgotten. For the brothers and sisters, the older ones were a shield between them and danger. But they never spoke of this, neither the big ones nor the little ones. That was why the older ones didn't know how much they loved their brothers and sisters. For if the older ones were finding it more difficult to put up with the younger ones now, it was because they themselves were ceasing to be inseparable from them, and because the whole lot of them no longer formed one single entity, one great machine for eating and sleeping, shouting, running, weeping, and loving, and were less sure of being able to guard one another against death.

The secret they shared was that they couldn't take things for granted as other children could. They knew that, separately and together, they were a disaster for their parents. The older ones never talked to them about this any more, ever, nor did the parents, but they all knew it, the youngest as well as the oldest. When the mother and father sent the older ones on errands, they never left the little brothers and sisters behind with the parents. Especially not the very youngest ones. They preferred to drag them around with them in ancient strollers, or to let them take a nap in the woods. The thing they feared most was leaving the youngest ones with the mother, in case she might take them to the social security office and sign the famous paper for selling children. You could never get them back again afterward. No one could. Not even the mother.

When the little ones got strong enough to escape, to run faster than the father, the older ones weren't afraid for them any more, because the parents would have their work cut out to catch them, it would be like trying to catch fish in a mountain stream. Five years old was the crucial age.

Ernesto and Jeanne knew the mother had such desires within her. The desire to abandon. To abandon the children she'd created. To leave the men she'd loved. To go away from the countries she'd lived in. To drop everything. Go off. Disappear. And they also knew she knew nothing about it. At least, that's what the children thought. Above all Ernesto and Jeanne, as if they knew it *for* her better than she knew it herself.

No one, either among those closest to her or in Vitry as a whole, knew where the mother was from, what part of Europe she hailed from or to what race she belonged.

Only Emilio had some inkling, and what he knew first and foremost about her life was what she herself didn't know. People in general thought she must have had another life once, before Vitry. Before she came here, to France, to this town and its hills.

She herself, the mother, didn't say anything. It was quite simple—never anything about anything. She was extremely clean, like a girl, washed every day; but she didn't say anything. She was very clever, but her intelligence couldn't ever have been used at all, either for good or ill. Perhaps she was still asleep, still in a kind of darkness; that was another possibility.

Yet sometimes she would start to talk. And what she said was always strange. It had happened long ago. It seemed insignificant. And yet it was something you remembered for ever. The words as well as the story. The voice as much as the words. And so it was that once, late at night, after she'd come back from the cafés in the town center, the mother told Jeanne and Ernesto about a conversation. It was, she said, the clearest, brightest memory in her whole life, and she still thought about it now, that conversation overheard by chance on a night train in Central Siberia, a long time ago now, she was seventeen years old at the time.

They were two ordinary-looking men, the sort you see anywhere. It was obvious they'd never met before this journey, and that they'd probably never meet again. The first thing they discovered was how far their villages

were away from each other. And then the younger one
had started to talk about his job as a public official, and
then about his present life, and he'd spoken too about
the darkness, the cold, and the beauty of the Arctic. Then
suddenly the conversation flagged. The younger man
couldn't speak of his happiness with his wife and children.
Then the older man talked about himself. He was a public
official too, like almost all the people who lived on the
plains of Siberia, and he too talked about the perpetual
night of the Arctic, and the cold. He had children too.
And he too talked shyly, as if such subjects weren't really
serious, about the silence of the polar night, the simulta-
neous silence and cold. Sixty degrees below for three
months of darkness. The younger man spoke of how
strangely happy the children were in that land of sledges
and dogs.

It was chiefly the way they spoke of these things that
was decisive for the mother. They spoke quietly so as
not to disturb the rest of the passengers, and didn't notice
that the others were listening with passionate interest.

For years the mother had remembered the names of
their villages. Now she'd forgotten them. But she did
remember the blue of Lake Baikal amid an immensity of
snow.

After that journey, the mother said, she'd gone and
made inquiries about the train services in Siberia. In order
one day, perhaps, you never knew, to go and see. See
the younger man's wife, she said, his house, the acres of

snow and stone all around it, the cattle cooped up for months in the cow sheds, the smell of darkness stuck fast in winter.

In Vitry the mother didn't want to have to converse either with the people of Vitry or with the members of her family. Except for Ernesto, she wanted to remain a stranger to those around her, even to Emilio, whom she still loved.

Except for Ernesto.

There was nothing unforgettable in the mother's life except those night trains bearing along an inexpressible happiness, those trains and her child Ernesto.

Ernesto was the only one of her children who was interested in God. Ernesto had never uttered the word God, and it was through the omission that the mother guessed something of the sort. God, for Ernesto, was the despair he always felt when he looked at his brothers and sisters, his mother and father, the spring, or Jeanne, or nothing. The mother discovered Ernesto's despair by accident, so to speak, when she saw him standing one evening looking at her with that look of his, always anguished and sometimes blank. That evening the mother realized that Ernesto's silence was at once God and not God, a passion for living and a passion for dying.

Sometimes, when she woke up, the mother would find the boy sleeping at the foot of her bed. Then she knew there had been a storm and a strong wind over Vitry during the night, and that the commotion in the sky had made a terrible noise. Whenever there was a storm, Ernesto would count the things God destroyed in the course of the night. A neighborhood, a road, or an apartment building: it was as if Vitry were being destroyed stone by stone. Ernesto was afraid. Once he told her he'd heard the commotion in the sky over the old highway where the children were forbidden to go. I swear it, he said, it was over there.

Apart from that, winter or summer, the mother wouldn't let the children into the kitchen except at mealtimes. Several times there were complaints: newcomers to Vitry were outraged that children should be treated like that. Out of doors all day and not sent to school. But the complaints were never carried through. The mother would say: What do you want me to do—hand them over to the state? Then the people would apologize and go away, scared.

It seemed to the brothers and sisters large and small, clearly or otherwise, that the mother fomented some inexpressibly important work inside herself every day, and that this was why she had to surround herself with silence and peace. She was heading for something—everyone knew it. That was what the work was—the future in the making, at once visible, unpredictable, and strange. What the mother was doing seemed without limit to others

42

because it hadn't been named, it was too personal. There weren't any words for it, it was too soon. Nothing could contain its whole contradictory meaning, not even the word that might have been applied to it. But in Ernesto's eyes the mother's life might have been a work already accomplished. And it might have been that work, held back within her, that caused the chaos.

The fact that the mother could scarcely write gave her work a kind of immensity. Everything contributed to the greatness of her work, as rainstorms go to swell the sea—the children she wanted to sell, the books she hadn't written, the crimes she hadn't committed. Also that other time, in the other Russian train, that lover lost in winter and now wiped out by oblivion.

Yes, there'd been that other journey, that other time, in another night train crossing Central Siberia. The time of the love affair.

What she was doing on the train the mother had forgotten. But not the love affair, not yet, she said, not quite yet, not as long as she lived, she'd say, that burning feeling in her heart, she'd always have that whenever she remembered, she could feel it at once there in her body.

The mother was already on the train when the man got on. They loved each other as long as the journey lasted. She was seventeen. In those days she was as beautiful as Jeanne, she said. They said they loved each other. They wept together. She lay down and he covered her up with his coat. The compartment stayed empty, no other passengers came in. Their bodies didn't part from each other all night.

It was after she got back from the bars in Vitry one night that the mother spoke about that journey. For months—more, for years, she'd waited to meet the man on the train again. She still thought of the waiting as part of the happiness she'd had with him. That night stood out in her life as dazzling, peerless. Their love had been so great the mother still trembled at it that night in Vitry.

The children would remember all their lives the time when the mother told them. They were all there, Jeanne and Ernesto and the brothers and sisters. While she was speaking the father was asleep in bed. He had all his clothes on, and his summer shoes, and he was breathing heavily, sleeping as peacefully as if he were lying in a field.

Just before dawn the train had stopped at a little station. The man woke up with a cry, seized his things, and got off as if in terror. He didn't come back.

Just as the train started up again he turned round toward it, toward the woman at the lit-up train window.

It lasted a few seconds. Then the train ran over his image on the station platform.

After collecting their family allowances, the father and mother used to go into the town center and drink Beaujolais and Calvados. They drank until midnight, when the bars in the town center closed. Then they'd go down to the Port-à-l'Anglais and the bistros on the quays. After that, if they couldn't find anyone to give them a ride home, they sometimes went up the Vitry slopes to the truck drivers' stop on the old N7 highway. They didn't always do this. But when they did it was four o'clock in the morning when they got back à la casa. So then, yes, the brothers and sisters would be desperate. They couldn't help fearing this was it, and now they'd never see those parents of theirs again.

For the children, death was not seeing their parents any more. Their fear of death was the fear of never seeing their parents again. The children knew they wouldn't die of hunger. Because if ever the parents stayed out late on one of their excursions into the town center, or the mother suddenly decided to go to bed and not get any more meals ready, Ernesto used to cook Quaker Oats for the children, and Jeanne would sing "A la claire fontaine." And Ernesto would say, There you are, now perhaps you'll stop yelling, you little dopes.

Sometimes, at night, when the parents were dead drunk, violent and incomprehensible things happened to them. One day they were found at the Porte de Bagnolet. Why the Porte de Bagnolet? They never knew. They were brought back to Vitry in a police van. After that escapade the parents stayed in their room for three days, they wouldn't let the children in or even answer them. Jeanne wept and hurled insults at them, she yelled that she'd kill them. Open the door or else I'll burn the casa down. Jeanne's voice was shrill, unbearable. All the children were crying. Ernesto took them out to the shed. Then in the end the father opened the door. He looked so desperate, Jeanne rushed out to the shed with her face buried in her hands. Ernesto went over to her. And she said maybe they'd been wrong, and if the parents really wanted to die as much as that they ought to be allowed to get on with it.

Sometimes the parents would suddenly shut themselves up in their room without having been to the town center. No doubt they did so for some reason that couldn't be explained, it was so specific and personal. Ernesto said perhaps it was the spring, the month of May. He remembered it had been the same the year before, and the year before that. Perhaps it was because of the cherry tree being in flower, the excessive spring that the mother said she couldn't bear any more, didn't want to look at any more. What got her down was the way spring kept coming around. Everyone else in Vitry rejoiced in the weather, so fine, so blue; and she, the mother, hurled insults at the flowering cherry. Filthy thing, she called it, and yet she wouldn't let anyone chop it down, wouldn't even let them trim off the little twigs that came in through the kitchen window.

Once Ernesto said to Jeanne that maybe they'd got it wrong, and perhaps it was to make love that the parents shut themselves up in the bedroom.

Jeanne didn't say anything after Ernesto said that. He looked at his sister for some time, and she had to shut her eyes. Then his eyes had wavered, and they too had closed. When they could have looked at each other again, they avoided doing so. In the days that followed they didn't speak. They didn't name this new thing that had shattered them and bereft them of speech.

It was shortly after that day that Ernesto read the brothers and sisters the passages from the burned book that related the doings of the son of David, king of Jerusalem.

—I built me houses, reads Ernesto.
—I planted me vineyards.

—I made me gardens and orchards, and I planted trees in them of all kind of fruits, reads Ernesto.

—And I made me pools of water.

Ernesto stops reading. The book slips out of his hands. He lets it fall. He looks exhausted. Then he goes on. This time without the book.

—Pools of water, Ernesto continues, to water therewith the wood that bringeth forth trees.

Ernesto stops. Is silent. He looks at Jeanne, who is lying against the wall. She opens her eyes and looks back at him.

And then Jeanne lowers her eyes again. It's as if she'd gone away from Ernesto again. But Ernesto knows that behind her eyelids it's him she sees and is seared by. Ernesto reads with his eyes closed so that he, likewise, may have Jeanne in him.

—I had great possessions of great and small cattle above all that were before me in Jerusalem.

Ernesto opens his eyes again.
He lies down. Tries to tear his eyes away from Jeanne's body lying against the wall.

—I gathered me also silver and gold, and the peculiar treasure of kings and of the provinces, Ernesto goes on.

—I gat me men singers and women singers, and the delights of the sons of men.

—So I was great, and increased more than all that were before me in Jerusalem; also my wisdom remained with me.

Ernesto looks as though he'd fallen asleep. But he shouts. It's as if he had fallen asleep and were shouting in his sleep.

—Whatsoever mine eyes have desired I kept not from them, shouts Ernesto.
—I withheld not my heart from any joy. Any love.

Ernesto straightens up. Picks up the book again. At first he doesn't read it. He's trembling. Then he starts reading again.

—Then I looked on all the works that my hands had wrought, and on the labor that I had labored to do: and behold, all was vanity and vexation of spirit. Vanity of Vanities. Chasing the wind.*

The children listened eagerly to what the King of Israel had done. They asked where they were now, these people, the Kings of Israel.

Ernesto said they were dead.

How? asked the children.

Gassed and burned, Ernesto said.

The brothers and sisters had probably heard something about this before. Some of them said: Oh yes . . . that's it . . . we knew about that.

Others wept, as they had when the book was found.

Then they came back to the rain and the pools. The things they liked best in all creation.

One brother said: I like it best when he plants the forests. What he couldn't understand was how you could *make* pools of water.

Another one said it was rain. The king put rain into pools, and then watered the forests and gardens with it.

The brothers and sisters were amazed at the king's cleverness.

They weren't too sure what vanity was. One sister thought it was when you wore dresses that were too

*The French translation corresponding to "vexation of spirit" in the King James version. *Tr.*

fancy and spangled. Another sister said: And with rouge all over your face as well.

None of the brothers and sisters knew what vanity of vanities was. About chasing the wind they had some idea, because of the great carcass of the deserted highway at the bottom of the slopes of Vitry.

Ernesto said the wind was also something else called knowledge. Knowledge was a kind of wind, both the wind that swept along the highway and that which swept through the mind.

One of the older brothers asked what knowledge was like, what knowing would look like if you tried to draw it.

Ernesto says: You can't draw it. It's like a wind that never stops blowing. A wind you can't catch, that never stops, a wind of words, of dust, you can't represent it, or write it down, or draw it.

Jeanne looks at Ernesto. She laughs too. When Jeanne laughs all the brothers and sisters laugh.

Is there a lot of knowing around? asks a very small brother.

People think there's quite a lot, says Ernesto, but they're wrong.

How much? asks the small brother.

Zilch or thereabouts, says Ernesto.

The very small brother is cross. He says *he* knows a little girl in Vitry, she's black and comes from Africa. Her name's Adeline Administrative.

A middle brother starts crying and yells:

You're crazy, Ernesto. Nuts.

Ernesto laughs. Then Jeanne does too. Then all of them.

Then Ernesto asked them not to forget that the last kings of Israel, in Vitry, were their parents.

When spring came the children turned golden pink and so did their hair, it turned a reddish blond, almost pink. They were very beautiful. Some people in Vitry said: What a pity . . . such lovely children . . . you'd never think . . . What would you never think, they were asked. That they were neglected, they answered.

The mother and father met in Vitry, which was where Emilio Crespi had settled when he arrived in France from Italy. It was there too that he got a job as a bricklayer with a building firm. He lived in a hostel for Italians near Vitry town center.

For two years Emilio Crespi lived alone, and then he met the mother, when she came, alone and twenty years old, to the hostel's annual party.

Her name was Hanka Lissovskaya. She was from Poland. But she wasn't born there. She was born before her parents went to Poland, she'd never found out where, in a village, her mother said, somewhere amid the jumble of peoples between the Ukraine and the Urals.

It was in Cracov that she'd met the Frenchman who brought her to Paris. But she left him as soon as they arrived, she never said why. To get away from him she walked for two days. She found herself in Vitry, and there she stopped. She went to the City Hall to rest and ask for work. Twenty years old, a reddish blond with sky-blue eyes and a Polish complexion. They gave her a job right away.

He was handsome, Emilio—dark, slim, bright-eyed, cheerful and gentle, charming. The very same night, the night of the party, she went to his room. They'd been together ever since.

She went on working as a cleaner at the City Hall until she had her first child. After the City Hall she never went out to work again. Emilio Crespi went on working as a bricklayer until the third child was born. After that he didn't work either.

With the mother, it wasn't that she was beautiful, it was something you couldn't put into words exactly. A kind of way of being beautiful, of knowing it, yet of acting like someone not beautiful. Of forgetting she knew she was beautiful, of treating herself badly, of not being able to help it.

For a long time the mother's past was painful for the

father to think about. For a long while he wondered who she was, this woman who had entered his life like a thunderbolt, like fire, like a queen, like a wild happiness chained to despair. Who was it in the house? Close to his heart? Close to his body? Nothing, the mother never said anything that threw any light on her youth, that obscure inexpressible past that was doomed, all unknown to her, to cause some day such suffering.

And then one day the children came. Each one of them was an answer to the father's question, Who was this woman? This woman was their mother, and their father's wife. His lover.

The father's pain left him when the children were born. And then later on they brought him much other pain. This new pain the father accepted.

School. The classroom. The teacher. He is sitting at his desk. Alone. No pupils. Enter Ernesto's parents. They all say hello to one another.

All: Bonjour Monsieur. Bonjour Madame. Bonjour. Bonjour Monsieur.

Silence.

Father: We came to tell you our son Ernesto doesn't want to go to school any more.

The teacher looks at the parents, blasé. The father goes on.

Father: We know we're supposed to send him to school, it's compulsory, so as we don't want to go to prison we came to conform . . .

Mother: Inform, he means, Monsieur. We came to inform you. Let you know.

Teacher: Speak plainly, Monsieur, please. Let's start again: you asked to see me to let me know what?

Father: Well, what I was just telling you . . .

Teacher: If I understand you correctly, you came to let me know that your son Ernesto doesn't want to go to school any more.

Parents: That's it.

Teacher, grandiloquently: But Monsieur, none of the four hundred and eighty-three children here wants to go to school. Not one. Don't you know that?

The parents are silent. They knew he'd say something like this. He laughs. So the parents laugh too. They don't say anything. They're not surprised. They laugh with the teacher.

Teacher: Do you know one single child who *does* want to go to school?

No answer from the parents.

Teacher: They have to be *made,* they have to be forced, they have to be pitched into, Monsieur. (No answer from the parents.) Do you hear what I say?

The parents are gentle and calm.

Mother: We hear, but *we* don't force children, Monsieur.

Father: It's against our principles, Monsieur. Sorry.

The teacher looks at the parents in astonishment, then he starts to smile because he's taken a liking to them.

Teacher: You must admit that's a good one . . .

The parents laugh with him.

Mother: The thing is, Headmaster, that in this case no one can force this particular child to go to school. Others, maybe, but him, no, no one could.

The teacher peers at the parents. He's comical. Suddenly he shouts.

Teacher: And why *can't* anyone force a child to go to school any more, may I ask? Why not? What a waste of time . . . I'm going crazy . . . I'm turning into a reactionary . . . (Pause.) I was under the impression I was speaking to you, Madame.

Mother: I'm sorry, Monsieur. I *was* listening . . .

The teacher has calmed down, he's enjoying himself.

Teacher: So we're not allowed to force kids any more, eh?

Silence. The parents exchange glances.

Mother: Well . . . you see . . . he's exceptional . . . He's very very tall . . . very very tall and very very strong.

Father: He looks twenty but he's only twelve. So you see . . .

Teacher: Yes . . . Oh dear . . . What can one . . .

Father: So you do see . . . For one thing, we can't get him out of the house. It's a physical impossibility, Headmaster.

Long silence. General weariness and waning of concentration. Silence.

Teacher, sorrowfully: And apart from that, how are things?

Mother: All right . . . How are things with you, Monsieur?

Teacher: Oh well . . . One keeps going . . . What else can one do?

Parents: That's right . . . One keeps going . . . and then . . . It's not too bad.

Teacher: Right.

Silence. The teacher remembers.

Teacher: In the present instance, it's very simple. We build a tiny little school all around him and he can't do anything else but stay there.

They all laugh. Then, all at the same time, they become serious again.

The mother turns first to her husband, then to the teacher.

Mother: But it's not just what you were saying, Headmaster, about him being so big . . . There's something else . . . The reasons he gives. That's very odd.

The teacher pretends to be very serious.

Teacher: H'm . . . Now let's be serious and methodical . . . I've got other things to do, you know . . . fifty-six pupils waiting for me . . .

Parents: Oh dear . . . as many as that . . .

Teacher: To start with: does your son Ernesto say *why* he doesn't want to go to school any more?

Father, after a pause: That's just it . . . He does . . . That's the trouble . . . As she was trying to tell you . . .

He says . . . Hold on to your seat, Monsieur. He says: I won't go back to school because they teach me things I don't know.

Teacher, after a moment's thought: I don't understand. I really don't.

Then all three burst out laughing. Then the teacher gets a grip on himself.

Teacher: It's a strange business though.

Parents: Certainly is . . .

Silence.

Teacher: What's he like?

The father gets slightly impatient.

Father: Tremendous. Really, how many times do you have to be told, Monsieur? . . . Small and tremendous.

Teacher: Sorry.

Mother: Dark. Twelve years old. Doesn't make much noise, though.

The teacher ponders. The parents watch him ponder. Silence.

Teacher: I see . . . Like trying to tackle a wild animal . . .

Mother: Oh dear . . . You haven't got it at all, Headmaster . . . Like trying to tackle nothing . . . Ernesto's not to be caught . . . It doesn't show . . . There's nothing there, you might say . . . It's inside, you see . . . On the outside he just looks, well, tall, but really it's all inside . . . concentrated, coiled up . . . You see, Headmaster, he's . . .

Father: It's obvious *you'll* understand, Headmaster—

it's written all over you ... There's no point in play-acting in the case of Ernesto ...

Mother, continuing as before: ... it just can't be done, Monsieur, ever ... he can't be made to believe things that aren't true, it's impossible, Headmaster ... *I* think it'd be better to kill him right away rather than ...

Teacher: What, Madame?

Mother: Nothing, Monsieur, nothing ... I'd better be quiet now ... I expect I'll be shedding tears over him before long ...

Teacher: I'm sorry, Madame.

Mother: No, *I'm* sorry, Monsieur ... He has to be left, Monsieur.

The teacher looks at the father and mother.

Teacher: Left where, Madame?

Mother: Where he is, Monsieur.

Silence. Peace is restored.

Teacher: Apart from that ... Does Ernesto give you any trouble?

The parents aren't frightened any more.

Father: Can't say he does.

The father looks at the mother.

Father: You agree, don't you ... We can't say he does ...

Mother: No. Can't say he does ...

The teacher catches their way of talking.

Teacher: Food? He eat too much?

Father: Eats pretty well, I'd say, eh, Eugenia?

Mother: Well . . . not really enough . . . He goes without so there's more for his mother and father and brothers and sisters . . . But nothing to worry about . . .

Teacher: Can you bring young Ernesto to see me?

Silence. The parents look at each other, uneasy again.

Father: What are you going to do to him?

The teacher adopts a man-to-man attitude with the father.

Teacher: Talk to him. Make him see reason. Appeal to elementary logic. Talk. That's the main thing. Talk. Defuse the crisis. Transfer it.

The father's dumbfounded at first. Then he nods toward the mother.

Father: So you haven't understood a word she's been saying . . .

Teacher: Not a word.

Once more the parents exchange anxious glances.

Father, after a pause: You mustn't be rough with him, Monsieur . . . Because if you were to try that . . . She's pretty strong . . . and she won't let anyone touch him.

Teacher: All right.

Silence. The teacher doesn't laugh. He ponders.

Teacher, looking at the parents: How is it I haven't noticed Ernesto more, seeing he's so tall? I don't understand.

Mother: Maybe you mistook him for someone else, Monsieur . . .

Teacher: Perhaps . . . He isn't nearsighted, by any chance?

Mother: No. Nothing like that. His eyes are very bright.

The father and the teacher look at the mother, both suddenly fascinated.

Teacher: Like yours, Madame.

Silence. The mother lowers her eyes.

Teacher: If you ask me I must have taken him for one of those Vitry loungers.

Mother: That's it . . . Don't bother to look for any other explanation, Monsieur.

Silence. General blankness. They look at one another. The teacher forgets. Then finally he speaks.

Teacher: Where are you from?

The father points to his wife.

Father: She's from the Caucasus . . . well, thereabouts . . . I'm from Italy. The Po valley . . . Yes . . . For generations . . . we used to come for the grape harvest . . . What about you . . . Monsieur?

Teacher, all in one breath: Seine-Maritime. The Caux area. Just up the creek from Bray.

The parents look at each other. They've never heard of it. Or of anything else. They know it.

They wait.

Time goes by. No one moves.

Father: Do you need us any more, Monsieur?

Teacher: No, no . . . That is . . . No.

More time passes.

The teacher is decidedly silent. He too is completely lost in some invisible subject.

Then in a low but clear voice he starts to sing the Alain

Souchon song "Allo maman bobo." The parents hear him out to the end, astonished. Then more time passes. And still no one moves.

Then the teacher goes to sleep.

The parents watch him sleep. And then finally they stand up. Very quietly—the teacher doesn't even notice. And then they creep out.

What made the children laugh was the father.

In the evening, at dinner. The way he kept saying certain things. Such as, There aren't any butterflies on me. Or, Money for old soap. The mere idea that the father might say something to make them laugh made them laugh. His expression whenever the mother's back was turned made them split their sides. He looked at her as if she were at once a mystery and a disaster.

In so doing he made himself seem like another of her children.

Once the father started making the children laugh there was no stopping them. Whatever he did to make them laugh they split their sides. Even if he didn't do anything they still split their sides. He would eat fried potatoes with a funny expression—as if to say, "What, again?"—and the children would split their sides. Once it had started, no matter what he did it set them off.

Sometimes the mother would start to sing especially

for the children. She'd sing the Russian lullaby "La Neva." She'd practically forgotten the words. And the father would join in in sham Russian. And then the mother too would howl with laughter, and the children, who didn't know any Russian, genuine or otherwise, would do the same. When the neighbors came round to see what all this crew were up to, one look and they were laughing too.

It was at such times, when the mother joined in with them and sang the lullaby, that the father and the children experienced their happiest moments.

And on those evenings, too, the mother took pleasure in the thought of her children, the idea that they were there cluttering up the time and space of her life.

As for the father, it was then, when the mother and all his children were roaring with laughter, that he believed what Ernesto said: that they were the happiest people in Vitry. The father's happiness was identical with that of his children. "I've got all I could wish for," he'd say. And the children would start to split their sides again, and he, as he laughed, would weep for joy.

But sometimes he would remind them that he was Italian, and came from the Po valley. "In case it hasn't sunk in yet," he'd say, "I'm from the Popo valley." And then all of a sudden he'd start speaking Italian, but an Italian the children didn't recognize, extremely fast and garbled, very ugly and dirty and coarse, and it poured out of him as if his last hour had come and he was ridding himself of all that remained of the other life he'd had before he was buried by this avalanche of children. When this happened the children would be frightened that the father might have gone crazy, and they'd throw themselves on him and thump him until he recognized who they were. So tell me who *I* am? You're the third, the father would say at last, you're Paolo.

Apart from that, the father didn't do anything. That's all there was to it. He was someone who'd eat potatoes cooked with onions every day without batting an eyelid. He collected the family allowances and his unemployment benefits. And no one, neither the mother nor the neighbors, found fault with the enormous unalloyed idleness he'd settled down into.

The father loved his children very much, but he accepted the system imposed by the mother. The children never entered the house of their own accord. Except Ernesto and his sister Jeanne. And it was another of the father's jobs to let the children know when it was time for dinner. He would whistle, and they would come running. They always washed their hands, the mother insisted on it, as she did on their taking a shower every morning. And then they fell to. Sometimes the mother wasn't hungry herself. But the father always ate with his children, and with just as hearty an appetite.

They talked about them in Vitry, especially the women, the mothers: People like that, they said, they always abandon their children sooner or later. What a shame, they said, such lovely children ... no schooling ... dragged up anyhow ... Other folks have offered to adopt some of them, but the parents won't hear of it ... That sort, they thrive on family allowances, if you take my meaning ...

Sometimes the children got wind of this gossip. It was then that Ernesto would say what the father believed. Let them talk, Ernesto would cry, we're the happiest children in Vitry. And through hearing Ernesto shout it aloud the children registered the fact of their dazzling happiness, like some wild animal leaping about in their heads, in their blood. Sometimes the happiness was so great it was terrifying to contemplate.

Ernesto and Jeanne slept in the corridor that separated the casa itself from the dormitory that the local authority had had built on to it. And so the brothers and sisters, shut away together with Ernesto and Jeanne, felt the older ones were still with them while they were asleep. Because what the youngest children feared in their minds was not that the mother might literally desert them, but that that she might cause them to be parted from her and from the father and from the other children. They already *were* deserted, in a way, and they knew it, but they also knew they were all deserted together. Being parted from one another was something they couldn't even imagine.

The children were the kind of people who could quite understand that they might be deserted. They understood things without actually comprehending them. They could understand desertion without actually comprehending it. It was only natural, really. Only natural that at some time or other parents should suddenly feel like deserting their children, just dropping them. After all, they themselves sometimes dropped their best marbles. But it was only natural, too, that they should cling to their mother and not want to let her go. The brothers and sisters could still remember the spaces of their earliest years. Daunting spaces, wild and unintelligible fears, of such things as deserted highways, storms, dark nights, wind. Who knows what the wind says, what it shrieks, sometimes. All the children's fears came from God, from that direction, from the gods. All the fears came from God, and thinking couldn't cure them because thinking was part of the fear. The children accepted being driven away, being deprived, they made no objection, they offered the mother no resistance. They loved her cruelty. They loved her. They loved being neglected by her. She was the cause of much of their fear. The brothers and sisters loved Ernesto and Jeanne almost as much as they loved the father and mother, but they knew Ernesto and Jeanne through and through and weren't at all afraid of them. Ernesto and Jeanne couldn't ever take the place of the sort of parents they had, especially when, as happened almost every day, the mother and father were angry with them and threatened to go away for ever to some country where the children couldn't reach them and where at last they'd be able to live unencumbered and without hope.

Another thing in all this was that the father couldn't bear to leave the mother alone all afternoon, à la casa or anywhere else. Nowhere did he dare leave the mother alone. He was always afraid she might run away and vanish for ever into some imperfectly imagined place that was a mixture of the bars in the port in Vitry, some vague frontier zone where France merged into the roads of Germany, and that other dim and shoreless zone in the center of Europe whence he supposed she came.

As the mother had the same fear about the father—that without her he'd disappear—they were always alone together à la casa in the afternoon, obliged in a way to keep watch on each other. Though they probably weren't aware of it.

Sometimes, all of a sudden, especially in winter, the father would miss his children and rush to the shed to see them, afraid he'd be too late and find they had vanished into the impenetrable maze of the suburbs—those suburbs amid which Vitry floated, now suddenly seeming light and frail, vulnerable and childlike and so itself delightful. But in winter the children were almost always there in the shed, because of the cold and the wind and fear. And in this the father would see again how abandoned they were. The shed was an image of the neglect for which he blamed himself. Sometimes he would weep and tell them why. It was because, he'd say, even though he loved them very much—and he knew this was so— he didn't love them as much as it was possible to love. He said this was because of the woman, their mother, whom he'd met on a train in Siberia, he said, and who'd taken possession of all the love he was capable of. The children never believed him when he talked like this, but he couldn't help accusing the woman he'd always been madly in love with, even before that night on the train in Siberia. Of course the father knew that loving several children was not the same as loving just one child, just one person, but his own children had given him a longing for a general love, and he now knew he'd never attain it because of his overwhelming preference, his insatiable desire, for this woman. She for her part resented being loved like that by any man, even the father of her children, because she knew, though she was the only one who did, that no one deserved to be loved like that by anyone. So the father lived in fear of losing a woman who was always telling him that one fine day, the finest day ever, she'd run away from him. And the father knew it was true, even after all these years he knew it was true. Ernesto knew too.

So the father loved the mother with the kind of unwavering passion usually directed toward some other object, a passion that scared her away and that was killing him.

What made her so lovable was the fact that she was unaware of her own attractiveness. And because her attractiveness derived from her lack of self-awareness, loving her was a desperate business. The father couldn't bear being alone with her and his passion and not being able even to tell her of it. And the children began to glimpse what the father's fate might be because of her, their mother.

Once one of the bigger little brothers said to the father: What you say isn't true, you didn't find our mother on the train in Siberia, it was someone else who found her, before you even knew her, you see what you're like, you'll say anything. The father didn't answer, not a word, but afterward he didn't talk any more about the mother's dreadful betrayal.

Once, long afterward, the father told Ernesto it was to please the brothers and sisters that he lied. Ernesto believed him.

After the mother told her children about the other journey, she talked to Jeanne about it. She said it was when they were in the earliest age of their desire that she told the father about the night on the train. For months the story made their desire fiercer. The mother hesitated: more dangerous, she said.

It was afterward that the father sullied the story of the train and turned it into a clue to the mother's character, tried to make her believe she was a prostitute, and wanted to kill her, kill their love, and then kill himself. Nothing else counted any more, not even the children.

Then one day the father stopped talking about it.

Often there were other children than the father's in the shed, not only children who were in their own mothers' way but also others, rich children. But when the father came, all the children were glad, his own and the others. And even when he wept in front of them, the children were glad even though they were sorry to see him "acting unhappy," as they put it. So that was what the father was like and that was how he lived, in the profound company of the children, in their ferocity and in their love.

The parents are afraid of the teacher. Emilio thinks any authority controlled by the State, even the most innocent-seeming, really has the weight of the law behind it.

As for the mother, since Emilio believes this so strongly she has come to believe it too.

So they take Ernesto to see the teacher since he's asked them to. Because when the teacher says anything, everyone believes him. And if he accused them of anything, he'd be in the right straight away, everyone would believe him without asking for any proof. He is the schoolmaster, master of the school and of the equipment and the children in it. So he can think whatever he likes. And if *he* decides there's no point in sending Ernesto to school, he can settle the matter accordingly. We mustn't miss the opportunity, Natasha.

The teacher's already there, in his big classroom, when Ernesto's parents arrive. He's sitting on one of the benches provided for the pupils. He's smiling.

Enter the father, the mother, Ernesto. And bonjour, Monsieur, bonjour, bonjour, bonjour Madame bonjour Monsieur, replies the teacher.

The teacher looks at these people, he's forgotten them. He looks surprised. He wonders why they've come. Then suddenly he remembers, when he sees Ernesto. The teacher and Ernesto look at each other.

Teacher: Are you Ernesto?

Ernesto: That's right, Monsieur.

Silence.

The teacher gazes intently at Ernesto. He does and doesn't remember.

Ernesto: I sat in the last row up at the back of the class, Monsieur.

Teacher: Oh, right ... I did recognize you ... but at the same time ...

Ernesto: I recognize *you*, Monsieur.

The mother gestures toward Ernesto, pretending to apologize for but really proud of him.

Mother: You see what he's like, Monsieur.

Teacher: I see.

The teacher smiles.

Teacher: So we refuse to learn, do we, Monsieur?

Ernesto looks at the teacher for some time before answering. How gentle Ernesto is ...

Ernesto: No, it's not that, Monsieur. We just refuse to go to school, Monsieur.

Teacher: Why?

Ernesto: Let's say there's no point.

Teacher: No point in what?

Ernesto: Going to school. (Pause.) It serves no purpose. (Pause.) Children who are at school are abandoned. A mother sends her children to school to learn that they're abandoned. That way she's rid of them for the rest of her life.

Silence.

Teacher: But you, Monsieur Ernesto, didn't need school in order to learn ...

Ernesto: Oh yes I did, Monsieur! It was there I realized. At home I believed all my stupid mother's rigmaroles. And then at school I was confronted with the truth.

72

Teacher: Which is?

Ernesto: That God doesn't exist.

Long and pregnant silence.

Teacher: The world's a botched job, Monsieur Ernesto.

Ernesto, calmly: Yes. You knew it all the time, Monsieur . . . it's a botched job.

Knowing smile from the teacher.

Teacher: Better luck next time . . . As for the present version . . .

Ernesto: As for the present version, let's say there's no point.

Ernesto smiles at the teacher.

Teacher: And so, if I understand you correctly, there's no point in going to school either . . . ?

Ernesto: That's right, Monsieur. No point in that either.

Teacher: And why's that, Monsieur?

Ernesto: Because there's no point in suffering.

Silence.

Teacher: So how do people learn?

Ernesto: They learn when they want to learn, Monsieur.

Teacher: What about when they don't want to learn?

Ernesto: When they don't want to learn there's no point in their learning.

Silence.

Teacher: How do you know God doesn't exist, Monsieur Ernesto?

Ernesto: I don't know. I don't know how one knows. (Pause.) Like you, perhaps, Monsieur.

Silence.

Teacher: And how, according to your system, does anyone learn if he won't learn?

Ernesto: Because there's no alternative, probably, Monsieur ... I think I must have known how it happens, once. And then I forgot.

Teacher: What do you mean: "I must have known"?

Ernesto shouts.

Ernesto: How do you expect me to know, Monsieur? You don't know yourself ... It sounds to me as if you say the first thing that comes into your head ...

Teacher: Forgive me, Monsieur Ernesto.

Ernesto: No, forgive *me* ...

Father: This boy! Where does he get it from?

Mother: Don't start, Emilio.

Father: All right ...

Silence.

The teacher and Ernesto smile at what the parents say. Then suddenly the teacher starts to shout, as if he'd just remembered his position.

Teacher, shouting: Education is compulsory, Monsieur! COMPULSORY!

Ernesto, amiably: Not everywhere, Monsieur.

Teacher: Here is here. We are here. This isn't everywhere, it's HERE.

Ernesto, pleasantly: You have to be told everything twice, it seems, Monsieur ... As everywhere is everywhere, here is everywhere too ...

Teacher: True.

Silence. Understanding and complicity are restored between the teacher and Ernesto. Mood of gentleness.

Teacher: And apart from that everything is all right?

Ernesto: Yes.

Teacher: What about your sister? She comes to school, if I'm not mistaken.

Ernesto: She did come to school, Monsieur—you're not mistaken . . . For four days.

Teacher: A lovely little girl . . .

Father: You can say that again . . .

Silence. Gentleness. Ernesto takes some pieces of chewing gum out of his pocket.

Ernesto: Would you like some chewing gum, Monsieur?

Teacher: Yes, please . . . Thank you, Monsieur Ernesto.

Ernesto gives everyone some chewing gum, his parents as well as the teacher. They all chew.

Mother, very sadly: To think it's come to this . . . he was such a clever boy . . .

She isn't laughing.

Ernesto, laughing: No, Mama. I'm not an idiot. And I won't become one, either. Why do you say that?

Mother: . . . I was saying it just for the others. I know you're not an idiot.

Silence. The parents join in with Ernesto, laughing. Then suddenly the teacher joins in too.

Father: That's no way to go on. You ought to give us the benefit of the doubt, Natasha.

Mother: I *did* try.

Father: Not so that *I* noticed.

Mother: It seemed to me I was trying.

Ernesto: Yes, you did try, Mama, I know. You're pretending you didn't now because of the teacher, but you did try, Mama . . .

Silence. They look at one another. Then they lower their eyes.

Teacher: You're very . . . very . . . Sorry—you're very nice people . . .

The father and mother look at each other doubtfully.

Father: Oh no, Monsieur . . . I'm very sorry. I don't know what we are. But nice . . . I don't think we're that.

Ernesto: It doesn't matter.

Teacher: That's right. It doesn't matter.

Silence. They look at one another.

Teacher, laughing: You're strange, too.

Mother: So where does that get us, Monsieur? Seven. We've got seven of them! And every day *I* feel I'd like to die . . .

Teacher, pensively: Yes . . . But this one, Madame . . . he's unique . . .

Father, conciliatory: There is that, you know.

Silence. They all chew gum.

Teacher: So what we have here is a boy who only wants to learn what he knows already.

Father: That's it.

Mother: No, he's never said that. He's quite willing to learn anything, anything, but what he doesn't know— no, he doesn't want to learn that.

They all do a slight double take and laugh, including Ernesto. Then they stop. Then they start to laugh again. And then stop again. Then Ernesto gets up. And the teacher says:

Teacher: What a lovely spring we've been having, though ... don't you agree ... ?

Mother: People always think that, Monsieur, but it's always the same.

Ernesto: I have to go, Monsieur. My brothers and sisters are hanging around somewhere and I must take them home. 'Scuse me, Monsieur ... You don't need me any more, Monsieur ...

Teacher: Well ... no ... perhaps not ... Please do what you have to do, Monsieur Ernesto ...

Ernesto: Thank you. Good-bye, Monsieur.

Teacher: Good-bye, Monsieur ... Perhaps we'll have the pleasure of meeting again ... ?

Ernesto smiles.

Ernesto: Yes ... perhaps.

Ernesto leaves. The teacher remains alone with the parents. They smile at one another.

Teacher: A surprising phenomenon, to say the least ... You don't see such things every day ... It makes a nice change ...

Mother: But you too, Monsieur ... I must say you're surprising, too ... I'd never have thought a teacher ... could laugh like you do ... Excuse me, Monsieur ...

The mother smiles at the teacher. The teacher suddenly sees her beauty and is astounded.

Father: But apart from that, Monsieur . . . What's to be done with children like that . . . later on . . .

Teacher: What you do, Monsieur, is let them do what they do do.

The parents remain. Are silent. The teacher is pleased, and the parents too have a comfortable feeling at being there with him.

Teacher: It was nice meeting . . . *I'm* delighted.

Silence. The parents haven't understood. They don't answer.

Mother: Now that you've seen him, Monsieur—Ernesto—I'd like to ask you something . . .

Teacher: Please do, Madame . . .

Mother: Will that lot be able to read one day, Monsieur, in spite of everything . . . To behave and eat and drink like everybody else?

The teacher grows serious. He answers very gravely.

Teacher: Without a doubt, Madame . . . Without the slightest doubt . . .

The mother is impressed. The father doesn't understand what's going on.

Mother: You're very kind, Monsieur . . . very kind . . .

Some time goes by. The mother and the teacher are both in the grip of the same emotion. The teacher realizes the mother knew he meant what he said.

More time goes by. No one moves. Then the father speaks.

Father: You don't need us any more, Monsieur . . .

Teacher, he's not sure, he's still feeling disturbed: No, Monsieur, no . . . That is . . . No.

Some time goes by.

And then the teacher starts singing Alain Souchon's "Allo maman bobo" again.

And the parents listen, just as enchanted as they were the first time.

And now the teacher has stopped singing. He forgets the parents. And falls asleep again.

The father and mother smile as they watch the teacher sleep, smile as if they were watching a child.

They stand up quietly so as not to disturb him.

And they go out of the classroom and across the empty yard.

But this time they make happily for the town center.

In the kitchen.

Afternoon.

The father and Jeanne are sitting on a bench facing the street.

We sense the father's inner disaster.

Father: Ernesto will never go to school again . . . As you know . . .

Jeanne is silent.

Father: Just once, and that was it. The teacher said it was all right . . .

Jeanne doesn't look at her father.

Father: I wanted to tell you . . .

Jeanne has stopped listening, she doesn't move.

Father: I feel beat . . . as if I were at my last gasp . . .

Jeanne has stopped listening, stopped moving.

Father: I wanted to ask you . . . *you* don't go to school any more either . . .

Jeanne: No. You know, so why do you ask?

Father: I want to hear you say it.

The father is very gentle. Cautious.

Father: I was sure it'd happen one day.

Silence.

Jeanne: What?

Father: Disaster.

Jeanne, shouting: It's not a bad thing really.

Silence.

The father pretends not to have heard.

Father: You missed Ernesto . . . that's it . . .

Jeanne doesn't answer. The father goes on with his long lament.

Father: Once you've known him you miss him when he's not there . . . What a nice boy he is . . .

Jeanne watches him weep. She doesn't cry.

Father: Which one are you?

Jeanne: I'm Jeanne.

Father: Our third . . .

Jeanne: No, your second. I'm the same age as Ernesto.

Father: How did you manage to get out of school?

Jeanne: I stood up and went out of the classroom. Then I strolled across the playground. The headmistress was on duty there, she saw me and smiled but she didn't say anything. Then I started to run.

Father: Would you believe it! . . .

Silence.

Jeanne looks outside. Ernesto goes past the kitchen.

Jeanne: There he goes, our famous brother.

Silence. Jeanne watches Ernesto go by. The father watches her. It's then that fear suddenly grips him.

He must be looking for me, says Jeanne. He's going to the dormitory . . . Look . . . He's coming back. He's turned around.

He's going to go back across the yard . . . After that he'll go to the shed.

Look, he's going there now, says Jeanne.

The father doesn't move. He looks at his daughter, has eyes for nothing else. In the face he once knew so well there is a strange, unbearable light. In her eyes as she looks at her brother.

After he's looked in the shed, says Jeanne, he'll go and look on the roads, as far as the highway. Until he finds me . . . All night he'll look for me if necessary . . .

Silence. Jeanne is silent. It's as if she were waking up.

Jeanne: Where is she? Where's Mother?

Father: I don't know. I don't know any more.

Jeanne: It's since you went to see the teacher.

Father, hesitating: Since then she's lost interest in everything. She says Ernesto's going to leave us some day or another. And she says *she'd* rather die.

The father weeps.

Father: What do *you* think?

Jeanne: I agree with her. Ernesto has no choice.

Silence. The father weeps. Jeanne looks at the road Ernesto has to cross after he's been to the shed.

Father: Has he said anything to you about it?

Jeanne: No. He doesn't know.

Father: You know for him.

Jeanne: Yes. He's going to leave us. He's going to leave everything.

The father avoids looking at her.

Father: He won't go away from you. Even if he leaves you he won't go away from you . . .

Jeanne: I don't know. There are some things that can't be said.

Silence.

Father: Are you done for too?

Jeanne laughs suddenly, and weeps at the same time. And then she shouts.

Jeanne, shouting: Don't you understand anything? I'm happy . . . it's marvelous . . . I'm wildly happy.

The father lets out a kind of wordless howl.

Father: Even if it'll kill you . . . not to go with him?

Jeanne: Even then . . . I'm happy.

The father, appalled, rushes away so as not to have to hear any more. While Jeanne sobs with the happiness of Ernesto, and softly calls to him.

Around Jeanne and Ernesto's happiness, the pattern of the family has been disturbed. The father stays away from the mother and the children. He goes and weeps in the cafés in the town center. He goes to the shed to weep too. And in the bushes by the highway, he goes there and lies down and weeps.

It was there that Jeanne went to look for him. He was weeping as he slept.

Jeanne sat down opposite him in silence and he woke up. He was rather ashamed of himself, and apologized. He told her he was suffering now as much as he'd suffered sometimes because of the mother when they were young. And he told her not to take any notice, because the pain would pass just as the pain the mother caused him had done.

He must have been to the town center, he's rather drunk. He looks at Jeanne with the same terror as when she confessed her terrible happiness. Gazes with all his might. As if looking at her was going to be the cause of his death. He sees what no one but he can see—that unknowingly, gloriously, terrifyingly, she has said good-bye to her childhood.

You're as wild as your mother, he said. Just as wild as she is.

Jeanne smiled.

The wind has dropped. There aren't so many cars going by on the highway now. The light from the street lamps hangs motionless over the waste of black concrete. Jeanne gazes at the light.

And then the father shut his eyes and breathed a woman's name:

Hanka Lissovskaya.

Jeanne looked up. Now *she* was suddenly frightened, scared by the stranger now visible in the father. She took her hand off his. He didn't move. He went on:

You're as beautiful as Hanka Lissovskaya. And as wild.

Who's she? cried Jeanne.

Your mother when she was twenty.

Jeanne spoke her mother's name for the first time, and wept with the father as they both worshiped life.

The kitchen. The cherry tree outside. Ernesto is by the window. The unwavering light of high summer. The mother is looking out. Ernesto comes up to her. Sits down facing her.

Mother: The teacher came. He said he wanted to speak to you.

Ernesto doesn't answer.

Mother: He said he'd thought it over. And your argument doesn't hold water.

Ernesto: My argument? I haven't got one . . .

Mother: You're angry today, Ernesto.

Ernesto: A bit.

Mother: Because of God still?

Ernesto: Yes.

Silence.

Mother: The teacher said that if all the children left school he'd just have to pack up and go.

Ernesto: All the children haven't left school. The only one who's left school is me.

Mother: You're cross with me too, Vladimir.

Ernesto: Yes. With you too.

Silence. Ernesto immensely gentle.

Ernesto: I didn't mean you. You can annoy me as much as you like, be as stupid as you want. I didn't mean anything in particular.

Silence.

Mother: Why do you love me like that, Ernesto, it's irritating, it really is.

Silence. They look at each other.

Ernesto: I don't quite know. Perhaps because I know you so well . . . There's nothing I can compare you with. You're better than anyone else in the world.

Mother: Not better than Jeanne.

Ernesto: The same. I didn't know until you said it.

Mother: Don't be under any illusions, Ernesto—I'm not like the driven snow.

85

Ernesto: I know that too. And you can be nasty as well.

Mother: Yes. And I ought to tell you I've never cared about moral qualities. Did you know that? . . . All I'm interested in is material possessions.

Ernesto and the mother both laugh and cry at the same time.

Ernesto: A nice bike? Is that what you mean?

Mother: Yes. A nice bike's a help. A nice fridge, some nice central heating. And some money. But I haven't got anything. You're the only positive thing in my whole life, Ernesto.

Ernesto: Once I used to think that when I grew up I'd get you all those material possessions. But I don't think so any more. You can't keep up with your parents.

Silence.

Mother: I'm not very interested in life . . . Never have been, really . . . Did you know that too, Ernestino?

Ernesto: With you, I've always known something like that, yes . . .

Silence.

Ernesto: I'm very sorry, Mama. Parents—when you might be able to give them something they're too old, they don't want to be burdened with things any more . . . So relationships always lag behind. I wanted you to know, Mama, that I grew up fast on purpose to try to catch up on the difference between us. Between you and me. But it wasn't any good . . .

The mother looks at her crazy son.

Mother: You really are tremendous, Ernestino . . .

Ernesto: If I wanted I could pass for a child who's as good a philosopher as a man of forty. I could earn my living like that if I wanted. You needn't be afraid any more of going without.

Mother: You think so . . .

Ernesto: Yeah.

Silence. Ernesto averts his eyes from his mother's.

Ernesto: By the way, where are my brothers and sisters?

Mother: At the circus, poor things.

Ernesto: So they are.

Mother: Yes.

Mother: Had you forgotten?

Ernesto: Almost.

Mother: Why aren't *you* at the circus?

Ernesto: Because I've never been interested in circuses, Mama . . . I was bound to have to tell you sooner or later . . .

Mother: It's true that whenever they brought on the lions you did a nose-dive . . .

Ernesto: That's right . . .

Mother: What are you doing now, Ernestino?

Ernesto: Chemistry, Mama.

The mother looks at her child, suddenly shocked.

Mother: Chemistry . . . Do you understand chemistry now?

Ernesto: At first you understand just a little bit . . . something . . . and then the lot. To start with it takes a long time, and then one day you understand everything. All of a sudden. It's staggering.

Silence.

Mother, trying to remember: How long is it since you stopped going to school, Ernesto . . . ?

Ernesto: Three months. You know what I do, Mama? I go and stand outside schools, and I listen to what's being said inside. And then I know. Just like that.

Mother: Good gracious, Ernesto . . . Oh my . . .

Ernesto: I'm in the fresh air. And it's quicker. You can do all the years at once . . . It's great . . . You mustn't worry, Mama.

The mother is appalled.

Mother, in a whisper: You've done all the years in the schools in Vitry in three months, Ernesto!

Ernesto: Yes, Mama. And now I must go on to Paris and the universities . . . It's obvious.

Now the mother's crying.

Mother: Let me look at you, Ernesto.

Ernesto, shouting: Don't cry, Mama, *please* don't cry!

Mother: I'm not, I've stopped now . . .

Ernesto: Don't think about Vladimir any more, Mama. Forget Vladimir.

Mother: All right. Forget Vladimir.

Silence.

They don't look at each other now. They look at the floor. Then Ernesto gets up from the bench.

Ernesto, after a pause: . . . Right, I think I ought to go and get my brothers and sisters. They're not easy to get hold of. They slip through your fingers . . . Real little fishes . . .

Ernesto has gone.

The mother's alone. She's dazzled, she's afraid, she weeps. Then she cries out. She calls Ernesto back.

Ernesto comes back and watches her weep, in silence. Then he says:

Ernesto: I wanted to tell you, Mama . . . I'm frightened too . . .

Mother, shouting: No . . . no . . . you mustn't, Ernesto . . . Not you . . . Not *you* . . .

When the brothers and sisters were very small, Ernesto used to say to them: If you cross the highway even once your mother will kill me.

And they'd never actually crossed it.

But every day for several months that year, the year of Jeanne and Ernesto, when the pain of seeing their beloved elder brother and sister drifting away from them was abating a little, the brothers and sisters still used to go and hang around by the highway, still from the quiet side of it, the side they lived on. Vitry-sur-Seine.

But the bigger ones, the ones who kept an eye on the small ones in the absence of Jeanne and Ernesto, were beginning to look at the other town, on the other side of the Seine, where they'd never been—they didn't even know its name.

And then one day that summer the brothers and sisters deserted the highway. That great empty hole of their childhood, that waste of black concrete—one day all the Vitry children abandoned it. Their fear of the forbidden highway had lasted too long and never been fulfilled, and all the Vitry children now waited—in despair, as they thought—for the black waste of their childhood to be destroyed.

Now it was up in the hills of Vitry that they sought adventure. Now it was in the rue Berlioz and the rue du Génie, in the streets named after Bizet, Offenbach, Mozart, Schubert, and Messager, in the courtyards of apartment buildings, in the paths between villas or the scrub on the slopes by the old highway, that they played at being afraid—as they once really had been—of losing one another in Vitry at night, or in Vitry in the daytime and emptied by the heat, motionless and devoid of its inhabitants, like something out of the readings from the burned book, the book about the gardens of the kings of Jerusalem, where it was never dark.

The father and mother are in the kitchen. They're alone. The light is softer now. The light there is at the end of a day in May.

Mother: ... It shatters me, Emilio ... (Pause.) You

know what he's on now? . . . Chemistry . . . All by himself
. . . He can read chemistry, and he can understand it . . .

Father: He only has to hear to understand. I've seen
him standing outside the Lycée Victor Hugo . . . Listening
. . . to a lesson on ether . . . $(C_2H_2)_2O$ . . . He didn't see
me. He was like a stranger.

Mother: A stranger . . .

Father: Yes.

Silence.

Mother: Emilio, I wasn't going to tell you, but the
lycées are all over and done with now too . . . Or will be
in two weeks . . . Now it's the universities . . . He's going
to Paris, to the universities . . .

Both fall silent. They're afraid. But they don't say so
any more. They're frightened at being afraid.

Father: Where's it all going to lead him . . . our boy . . .
our little boy . . . We mustn't cry any more, Ginetta . . .
It's better than if he were dead . . . that's what we have
to tell ourselves.

They're silent for some time. The mother's the first to
speak.

Mother, slowly: I've been wanting to tell you, Emilio
. . . I'm not crying just for the sake of crying, Emilio.
It's because my heart is full, too . . . I'm all upset . . .
Intelligence isn't our thing at all, and yet we've given
birth to it.

Father: I've been thinking about the others too . . . All
those little children . . . the whole string of them . . .

Silence.

91

Mother, consolingly: No point in grieving over *them*, Emilio ... They're still too young, and you never know ... Very likely *they* won't go striking out for themselves ... They'll stay here, live in Vitry, and so ... nothing to get excited about ...

Silence.

Father: You mean Ernesto's going to go away ...

Mother: You know he is.

Father: Far away from France.

Mother: Everywhere. You know that too, Emilio.

Father: Because of that knowledge ...

Silence.

Mother: Maybe the knowledge itself was fated.

Father: Stop it, Emilia ...

Silence.

Mother: The girl—she'll go too.

Father: She's the sort to go, too ... Jeanne ... It's unbearable ... Not to have her there any more ... It's impossible, terrible, terrible ...

The mother hesitates, then brings it out.

Mother: That's not the only thing, you know, Emilio.

The father says he knows.

More tears. The father's still weeping. The mother takes his hand to try to take away his suffering.

Mother: It's a very great happiness for me, Emilio.

Silence. All the father can do now is weep.

The mother takes Emilio in her arms. She turns her face away from his.

Mother: Listen, Emilio . . . If the girl's kept from Ernesto she'll do away with herself.

Silence. Then he asks with a groan:

Father: How can you know such a thing?

Mother: Because I'd have done the same if I'd been kept from you.

They embrace.

Father: It's so hard, Emilia. So hard . . .

Mother: There's nothing more we can do, Emilio. One day your children go away. You're bereft of them.

Silence.

Mother: I've got a confession to make, Emilio . . . When they were very small . . . there were times I'd have been in favor of abandoning them . . . I never told you.

Father: I suspected it sometimes . . .

Mother: I wanted to leave you. Never come back.

Father: You've always asked too much of life, Ginetta.

Mother: It wasn't that, Emilio. I don't know what it was.

Silence.

Mother: I still don't know now.

Ernesto and Jeanne have left the sisters and brothers in the alfalfa field. They themselves are on the path in front of the casa. The father and mother are watching them from inside the kitchen window. They can't hear what they're saying.

Jeanne: The teacher informed the Ministry of Education. The minister called in the mayor. There was another man from Paris, too. They talked it over and agreed they should send you to a school of higher mathematics in America. So you could become a professor.

Silence.

Ernesto: Who else was there in the kitchen?

Jeanne: Mother and me. Not Father.

Silence.

Ernesto: Did she say anything?

Jeanne: No. It'll be the same with Father. What could they say?

Silence.

Jeanne thinks they shouldn't tell the brothers and sisters about this.

It's still light. Jeanne and Ernesto don't rejoin their brothers and sisters. And they don't ask themselves why. They don't ask themselves anything any more. Once, before they knew, they sometimes talked about God. Not now. The not talking about God is because of Jeanne; now he hovers over the silence and has become a danger. Meanwhile they don't resist the need they have to be together all day and all night. Ernesto is alone with Jeanne. And Jeanne is now a young woman who says nothing, who is fierce, frightening.

What they know in the silence is that they are heading for an event that still seems a long way off but already seems inevitable. A kind of end, or death. Which perhaps they will not share.

That evening the children have left the hills behind and gone down the long slope leading to the highway. They come home at sunset. Just after they cross the road on the way to the shed, the father and mother cross it in the other direction. The father and mother are in the clothes they wear to go out. The mother's got her little blue hat on, the father's wearing the English cap he found on a train. They pass close by Ernesto and Jeanne without a glance, as if they hadn't seen them. They're arm in arm and walking quickly; they know there'll be some shouting and bawling from the shed. They go past it. By the time the brothers' and sisters' shrieks and yells reach them they're already on their way.

Ernesto and Jeanne join the brothers and sisters in the shed. We were here all the time, shouts Ernesto, you silly little dopes.

In the past Ernesto and Jeanne used to cry with the brothers and sisters whenever the parents went out to the town center.

They don't cry with them any more. One day all that came to an end.

The brothers and sisters cry more and more often, but

quietly. They don't complain any more. They leave the shed much less often, as if they were afraid danger and sorrow awaited them outside. But they never say anything about the reasons for the inability to live that threatens them. They also go to sleep more and more frequently in the shed. Jeanne has to go and get them and take them to the dormitory one by one.

Sometimes the brothers and sisters look like little animals huddled together in sleep, covered over with the gold of their hair, their little feet sticking out from under the heap. Sometimes they're scattered, like children dumped down anywhere. Sometimes they look a hundred years old, as if they'd forgotten how to live, how to play, how to laugh. They gaze after Jeanne and Ernesto as they go further away from the shed every day. They weep quietly. They don't say what it is they're crying for. Not a word. They say it's nothing, it'll pass.

The teacher has come to see Ernesto in the shed.

The teacher talks about the wonderful spring. Then he changes the subject.

Teacher: School, Monsieur Ernesto . . . Aren't you coming back?

Ernesto doesn't know how to put it.

Ernesto: Well ... It's a bit late for that, Monsieur ...
Silence.

Teacher: I know, Monsieur Ernesto. I knew as soon as I saw you ... I'm sorry, Monsieur Ernesto. But reading and writing, Monsieur Ernesto ... You've reached a very advanced, a very difficult stage ... The only problem is ... filling in the earlier stages.

The teacher is nervous. He smiles at Ernesto.

Ernesto: I'm sorry, Monsieur, but ... no ... I could read ... without knowing how ... before ... So you see ...

Teacher: But how ... I don't want to bother you, but ...

Ernesto: Well, I just opened the book and read ... You remember, don't you, Monsieur? The burned book ... so you could check that I hadn't got it wrong ...?

Teacher: Yes ... yes ... wasn't it a story about a king ...?

Ernesto: That's right ... That was how I knew I could read ...
Silence.

Teacher: Jewish. A Jewish king.

Ernesto: Jewish ...?

Teacher: Yes.
Silence.

Teacher: ... Yes. "Vanity of vanities, vexation of spirit, and chasing the wind."

Ernesto: Yes.

Teacher: Why the wind, Monsieur Ernesto?

Ernesto: The wind is the spirit, the mind, Monsieur— it's the same word.

Teacher: True. It's the same everywhere, I believe?

Ernesto: Yes.

The teacher is silent for some time. He looks at Ernesto. He's begun to be fond of both Ernesto and Jeanne, to love them with a strong and irresistible love.

Teacher: What about writing, Monsieur Ernesto?

Ernesto: That was the same, Monsieur. I picked up a pencil stub and just wrote. How do you explain that, Monsieur?

Silence.

Teacher: It's inexplicable. I can't understand it. How do *you* explain it, Monsieur Ernesto?

Ernesto: I couldn't care less about explanations, Monsieur.

Teacher: True.

Silence. They smile at each other.

They are silent for a while, as is their habit sometimes. Then the teacher speaks.

Teacher: What were the first words you wrote?

Silence. Ernesto hesitates.

Ernesto: It was for my sister.

Silence.

Ernesto: I wrote that I loved her.

Ernesto speaks very slowly, and as if he didn't see the teacher, as if he were alone.

Teacher, hesitates and then brings it out: But your sister ... at that time ... she was supposed not to know how to read or write.

Ernesto: She knew what I'd written on that piece of paper.

Teacher: How is that possible?

Ernesto: Perhaps she showed it to someone in the village. But I don't think so. I think she read it in the same way as I wrote it ... sort of without knowing, if you see what I mean ...

Teacher, hesitates and then brings it out again: You're right, Monsieur Ernesto. Jeanne could already read then.

Silence.

The teacher goes on rather more loudly.

Teacher: Like you, Monsieur Ernesto, Jeanne could read before she learned how ... Jeanne is you, Monsieur Ernesto ... You both spring from the same source.

Ernesto doesn't answer.

The teacher says that if Ernesto goes away, *he'll* see that Jeanne goes on with her studies.

Ernesto doesn't answer. He's becoming abstracted, as he always does when madness approaches.

Teacher: Forgive me, Monsieur Ernesto ... But what did you say in that letter? That you loved her more than she could imagine? ... That you loved her in a special way?

Ernesto: Yes. That I was in love with her. I told her I was in love with her.

Teacher, very quietly: I knew it. (He hesitates, he

smiles, he's overcome by his feelings.) I just wanted to hear you say the word.

Ernesto doesn't say anything. He's shattered: he never talked about Jeanne to anyone, not even his mother, not even Jeanne herself.

Ernesto comes back to the subject of the mother. He says the father taught her to read when they met, but she'd already had some lessons at the City Hall when she worked there. It was easy. Almost as soon as the father began to teach her she'd started to read books.

Ernesto and the teacher say nothing again for some time, then the teacher starts to talk about when he went to see the mother.

Teacher: I went to see your mother, Monsieur Ernesto ... Your mother's afraid, Monsieur Ernesto—did you know that?

Ernesto is suddenly worried.

Ernesto: Did she tell you so?

Teacher: No ... it was your father ... he phoned me ... What do you think she's frightened of, Monsieur Ernesto?

Ernesto: Of *my* fear, I expect, Monsieur.

Silence. Ernesto is a long way away, with his mother. He shuts his eyes so as to see her more clearly.

Ernesto: I think she's afraid because I'm afraid, Monsieur. Because I'm afraid too. I think she and I have the same fear.

Silence.

Ernesto: I thought I might find a way out in chemistry, a chink leading to the outside, an escape into the air. You see, Monsieur. But no. And my mother can see I'm starting to be afraid. She, for all her ignorance, has the same fear as I have.

Silence.

The teacher hesitates, then makes up his mind.

Teacher: About the burned book . . . Tell me, Monsieur Ernesto . . .

Ernesto, trying to find a way to put it: Exactly . . . with that book . . . it was as if knowledge took on a new aspect, Monsieur . . . Ever since entering into the kind of light that issues from the book . . . it's been like living in a state of wonder . . . (Ernesto smiles.) I'm sorry . . . it's hard to express . . . Words don't change their shape, they change their meaning, their function . . . They don't have a meaning of their own any more, they refer to other words that you don't know, that you've never read or heard . . . you've never seen their shape, but you feel . . . you suspect . . . they correspond to . . . an empty space inside you . . . or in the universe . . . I don't know . . .

They are silent. Then Ernesto comes back to his mother again and smiles. And says:

Ernesto: You see, my mother, who hasn't got any kind of book learning, none at all, she has this fear too. How do you account for that?

That evening the teacher stays there in the shed with Ernesto until it gets dark, until it gets cool and the children come home. Then, very politely, Ernesto tells the teacher he ought to go.

The teacher didn't apologize for staying on. Perhaps he didn't hear what Ernesto said properly. He started talking again. He said he was unhappy, he didn't believe in his job any more, it was one of those phases, he didn't believe in anything any more. Only their company— Ernesto's and Jeanne's and the brothers' and sisters' company—kept him alive.

It's pitch dark. The parents haven't come home. The brothers and sisters cried, but Jeanne switched the light off in the dormitory and they eventually went to sleep.

Ernesto's bed is outside the dormitory door. Like that, as soon as the sun rises, he can read the books the teacher gets for him, without waking the brothers and sisters.

Jeanne's bed is there too, near his own, in the same obscurity. The mother suggested this arrangement when Jeanne was still small, after they'd taken her to the clinic in Vitry. Because otherwise she might have tried to run away and set things on fire.

That night Ernesto approached the outskirts of Jeanne's body, the warm surface of her lips, of her eyelids. He looked at her for a long time. When he went back to bed he could hear the night sounds, the singing and laughter of drunks and young people, shouts, the din of police cars on the N7. Every so often the night sounds were swallowed up in silence. Silence in Vitry always came from the valley and the river. The trains murdered it, the noise took a long time to disappear, but then the silence returned like the sound of the sea. Ernesto forgot the parents somewhere out there in the town center. The night had come to belong to Jeanne.

The parents got back at about two in the morning. The mother was singing "La Neva." It was a great song, very beautiful, though it didn't have words any more. Jeanne was woken up by the sound of "La Neva," which she'd heard ever since she was born each time her parents came back from Vitry town center.

A lot of the people who lived in the villas along the way to Vitry town center knew the wordless "Neva," but couldn't remember where they'd heard it, whether on television or sung by immigrant children in the streets of Vitry. But plenty of non-immigrant children sang "La Neva" too. So they couldn't tell where it came from.

Ernesto too had heard the mother's magnificent voice emerging from the darkness. Without pronouncing a single word, the voice told the vast slow story of a love affair, of the love between the two lovers, and also of the splendor of the body of their child, the silent Jeanne now listening to "La Neva" in the dark dormitory. And the mother's "Neva" also told how difficult and terrible life was, how pure and charming they, the parents, were, and, she also said, how unaware they themselves were of it. Although, she said too, the children did know it.

At the mother's voice the night grew heavy with a wild and violent happiness that Ernesto suddenly knew he would never experience again.

That night Ernesto realized that his departure from Vitry was approaching, and that it was henceforth inevitable.

It was that same night that Jeanne slipped into Ernesto's bed and lay down close to her brother's body. She waited for him to wake up. It was that night that they took each other. Motionless. Without a kiss. Without a word.

The spring stretches out, slow and heavy, almost hot. It's another evening.

Summer Rain

The teacher's outside the shed. He looks inside. Ernesto and Jeanne and their brothers and sisters are there. Ernesto is reading aloud, slowly and clearly, the parts of the burned book that were left intact.

The brothers and sisters are listening with all their might.

The parents aren't there. The teacher, like all the people in this part of Vitry, must know about their passion for the town center. But he's already becoming unable to separate the parents from their children.

The teacher comes to see Ernesto in the evening. He brings chewing gum for the brothers and sisters. The parents aren't there, as usual—they're together somewhere away from the children. The teacher isn't very clear what it is he comes to see. He comes in fact for something he no longer tries to understand. He comes to see these people as he might go to another country, as if he were visiting an irresistibly lovely landscape that has nothing to do with the rest of Vitry and that is inhabited only by these people—the brothers and sisters and the older ones who look after them.

The teacher says that until he met this family he didn't know how attached you could get to children, how crazy about them.

The sister after Jeanne was Suzanna. After Suzanna came Giorgio. After Giorgio there was Paolo. And then Hortensia. And then Marco. He was five.

105

When he's free in the afternoon the teacher comes to the shed to teach the brothers and sisters to read and write. Jeanne comes to listen to the teacher's lessons too, while Ernesto is at the universities in Paris.

Ernesto knows about the teacher's lessons. He says he knew, that it was bound to happen sooner or later. He's always known the brothers and sisters would be able to read and write sooner or later.

The teacher often talks to Giovanna—as he calls Jeanne—and Ernesto about their little brothers and sisters.

Whatever the teacher tells them about the sisters and brothers, Giovanna and Ernesto laugh heartily. They laugh at everything, good and bad, that happens to their brothers and sisters.

The quickest learners, according to the teacher, were Suzanna and Paolo. Those he was fondest of were the two youngest, Hortensia and Marco. These two would come and sleep beside him during the lesson, to make sure of not losing him as they'd lost Giovanna and Ernesto and all the rest.

At the door of the shed stands the teacher, listening motionless to the story of the king. Ernesto's voice is slow and carefully articulated.

—The words of the Preacher, the son of David, king of Jerusalem, says Ernesto.

—I gave my heart to seek and search out by wisdom

concerning all things that are done under heaven: this sore travail hath God given to the sons of man to be exercised therewith.

Ernesto's voice is sometimes that of a child.

—I have seen all the works that are done under the sun, Ernesto goes on.

—And behold, all is vanity and vexation of spirit, chasing the wind.

—That which is crooked cannot be made straight: and that which is wanting cannot be numbered.

Ernesto rests for a moment.

—I communed with my own heart, saying, Lo, I have gotten more wisdom than all they that have been before me in Jerusalem: yea, my heart had great experience of wisdom and knowledge.

—And I gave my heart also to know madness and folly: and I perceived that this also is vanity and vexation of spirit. And chasing the wind.

Ernesto closed his eyes as if he was in pain.

The teacher moves closer to the shed and sees Jeanne is there, lying on the ground opposite Ernesto.

The teacher sees they're looking at each other in complete unawareness of the fact that he's looking at them.

He flees, he weeps with shock, he can't bear not being unaware any more, and yet at the same time not knowing.

The teacher has come back. Once more he waits outside for Ernesto, he doesn't go into the shed.

The voice that's singing is Jeanne's. I rested by the clear fountain ... The water was so clear I went in ... Long have I loved you, never shall I forget ...

The teacher is overcome by Jeanne's voice.

Ernesto has come to the door of the shed. He smiles at the teacher. He doesn't see that the teacher is weeping.

Teacher: Forgive me, Monsieur Ernesto ... once again I couldn't help coming ... when it came to be evening ... I haven't got anyone in Vitry, it's a wilderness, you're all I have.

Ernesto: But Monsieur, why shouldn't you come?

Ernesto comes over to the teacher. The teacher looks at him very fondly.

Ernesto: I just wanted to tell you, Monsieur, I've reached the last days of knowledge.

Teacher: What's that you say, Monsieur Ernesto? You've reached what?

Ernesto: German philosophy. I wanted to tell you ...

The teacher mutters to himself what Ernesto has just said.

Teacher: German philosophy ...

Ernesto: Yes. I shall stop soon now.

The teacher buries his face in his hands.

Teacher, crying out: I'm a criminal, Monsieur Ernesto ... You've gone crazy ...

Silence. Ernesto smiles at the teacher.

Teacher: But . . . isn't there anything after that?

Ernesto: I don't think so . . . I speak only for myself . . . It's only my own opinion . . . In my opinion there's nothing after that . . . nothing but mathematical deduction . . . merely mechanical . . .

Teacher, low cry: Nothing . . . that closes the cycle . . . as far as that aspect of things is concerned . . .

Ernesto smiles.

Ernesto: Or else it opens it . . . It's up to us, as you know very well, Monsieur.

Teacher: No, I don't know, I don't know anything . . . So what is left, in your opinion, Monsieur Ernesto?

Ernesto: All of a sudden the inexplicable . . . Music, for example . . .

Ernesto looks at the teacher very fondly, smiling.

The teacher smiles back.

The kitchen. A reporter has just arrived and is in the kitchen with Jeanne. He says he's from the *Fi-Fi littéraire.** Jeanne's never heard of it. The name makes her laugh.

---

*The allusion is to the literary supplement of the conservative daily *Le Figaro. Tr.*

Reporter: The foreign ministry got in touch with us ...
I believe you're Ernesto's sister? ... Jeanne? ... is that
the name?

Jeanne says yes, it is.

Reporter: Forgive me, I'm rather confused ... You're
so ... gorgeous ...

Jeanne laughs. Still at the name of the paper.

Jeanne: What did you say the name of your paper was?
The *Ri-Ri littéraire?*

The reporter laughs.

Reporter: No, the *Fi-Fi.*

Jeanne: I suppose it's for children.

Reporter, making a face: You could say that ... (Pause.)
I came to get your ... opinion ... about your brother.
Where does he get his ideas from? Have you got any
opinion on the subject?

Jeanne, smiling: No.

Reporter: You see ... I wondered whether it might not
be a put-up job ... a scam, as they call it ...

Jeanne: I don't understand what you're saying. You'd
better ask my brother ...

Reporter: I don't like to.

Jeanne smiles kindly at the reporter from the *Fi-Fi.*

Reporter: Forgive me ... I may have got it wrong ...
In which case it might be a kind of protest ... about
injustice ... immanent injustice ... the state of society
or something ...

Jeanne: I don't think my brother's interested in all that.

Reporter: I'm sorry . . . But . . . these things have to be said . . . Can you at one and the same time live off this society and expose it . . . the way it works . . . ?

She's beautiful, Jeanne. And she's not shy. She likes to laugh, and she likes to cry. She's lucid too. Like amber, the mother says. She says, politely still:

Jeanne: If that's what you've come for it's not worth waiting, we have no opinion about that sort of thing here.

The reporter takes Jeanne's mockery well. They start to laugh, both of them.

Reporter: Have *you* studied sociology?

Jeanne: Not much . . . Nor has Ernesto, but he's done more than I have.

The reporter is dumbfounded.

Reporter: Good grief . . . How old are you?

Jeanne: Ten, nearly eleven—a year younger than Ernesto.

The reporter looks at her and laughs heartily.

Reporter: Tell me . . . There's something funny in your family when it comes to figures. Eleven years old—don't tell *me!* Anyhow, no one in the village believes it. The fact is that you're making fools of everybody, and that's all there is to it.

Jeanne doesn't answer. She laughs to see the reporter from the *Fi-Fi littéraire* laugh.

Reporter: Forgive me . . . but . . . what do you get out of it? . . . all this?

Jeanne: It's difficult . . .

Reporter: How do you mean, difficult?

Jeanne, briskly: Difficult to say. Difficult to understand, too . . .

Silence. The reporter gazes at Jeanne for some time.

Reporter, now using the familiar *tu:* . . . Did you quit school too?

Jeanne: Yes. I didn't stay as long as Ernesto. Only four days. He stayed ten. That's not bad. I couldn't stand being away from Ernesto. We'd got as far as Popol. "Papa Punishes Popol." Do you know it? And Madame Chevalier.

Reporter: Listen . . . I've got to do an article . . . somehow . . . so . . . Just tell me anything you like . . . After all . . . To hell with the *Fi-Fi littéraire* . . .

Jeanne: Which would you like—"Papa Punishes Popol" or "Mama Modernizes her Manor-house"? I know the genuine texts.

Reporter: Let's have "Papa Punishes Popol."

Jeanne: Listen, then . . . you have to pay attention or you can't understand.

"Why does Papa punish Popol?"

But Papa never has punished Popol. The teacher made it up just so he can say "Papa punished Popol." But Papa's never punished Popol—never, never.

I don't know the end, says Jeanne.

The reporter finishes copying down what Jeanne has dictated. He reads it over under his breath as he writes: Po Pol. He starts to giggle.

Reporter: It's a bit on the short side ... Have you got anything else ... ?

Jeanne: There's "Madame Chevalier."

Reporter: OK, I'll buy "Madame Chevalier." Off you go ...

Jeanne: Here you are, then. "Madame Chevalier has a little dog called Riri one morning Madame Chevalier says to Riri we're going to the market it's a fine day she is very pleased she meets Madame Duverger and she asks how is your little girl then she meets Madame Stanley and then the concierge and every time she says something like oh my what a lovely day and then suddenly she sees some plums and she says oh I nearly forgot I came to the market to buy some plums dear me how forgetful I am why didn't you say something Riri but Riri sulks because he doesn't like fruit and Madame Chevalier knows that but she doesn't care she asks the man how much a kilo the plums are and the man says three francs and she says oh my what a price and she buys ten kilos.

Question: How much did Madame Chevalier pay for her ten kilos of plums?

The reporter bursts out laughing and Jeanne laughs with him.

Jeanne, laughing: ... That's all I know ...

Reporter: It's not every day you get to laugh like that in our lousy job. Especially at the *Fi-Fi littéraire,* which is a hundred years behind the rest of the world.

He looks at Jeanne.

Reporter: Do you ever go to Paris?
Jeanne says no, never.
He goes on looking at her.
Reporter: Have you got a sweetheart?
Jeanne smiles.
Jeanne: Yeah.
Reporter: Are you really eleven?
Jeanne: Yeah.

They reached summer abruptly, all of a sudden. As soon as they woke it was there, motionless, gloomy. The sky was a sinister blue, the heat already sweltering.

One morning, still very early, perhaps about seven, the whole of Vitry was filled with a deafening racket. The noise came from low down on the sides of the Seine valley.

The father said it was bound to come some day and now it had. It sounded as if he was talking about the heat.

In the previous few days Bouygue cement mixers had been seen coming down the N7, together with bulldozers, mechanical shovels, and German excavators. Generators followed. Last came buses full of workmen from North Africa, Yugoslavia, and Turkey.

And then, suddenly, silence. For the greater part of the day no more people or equipment arrived in Vitry. Until the evening. Then just before dark a new vehicle, a sort of mobile apartment block made of metal, a kind of tank of unknown power, arrived from along the N7 and descended very slowly toward the river. It came from a different country from that of the other industrial machines.

It was late in the morning that the destruction of the old highway began. The kill, as the father called it.

If the people of Vitry didn't know already what was afoot, when they heard the first hollow thuds they all realized this could only mean the final destruction of the old, black concrete highway.

On the evening of the first day, the mayor spoke to the population. He told them how the town was soon going to be developed so as to become competitive. The railway tracks would be moved to make more room for the new industrial estate. And the town was to be rid of the shantytowns down by the river, together with the brothels and bars that were a disgrace to the local working people.

He announced the construction of several public housing projects—the kind that had been promised for the last twenty years.

This final piece of news came as a shattering blow to the father and mother and Ernesto and Jeanne and the brothers and sisters.

For weeks the dying throes of the old highway shook the hills of Vitry, rattling the rickety buildings in the little streets running down to the port, the birds, the dogs, the children.

Then everything went quiet.

A new and echo-less silence descended. Even the sound of the sea had disappeared, along with the foreign communities driven from their homes on the banks of the river.

One evening, just like any other, when Ernesto comes home from Paris, there are two wicker garden chairs in the yard in front of the house. They've been set down by the untended hedge that runs around the yard on the opposite side from the cherry tree. The chairs look as though they'd just been left there side by side like that and forgotten, facing toward the street and watching people and bicycles and time go by. They're old-fashioned patio chairs, probably very expensive, very solidly made and very alien in this setting. The wicker shines as though it had been polished. Perhaps the chairs were actually cleaned before they were accidentally left there, or, who knows, put in front of the casa deliberately.

Nothing like this had ever happened before in the yard, not in the whole of the family's history.

While the chairs stand there, so real they seem unreal, Ernesto realizes there isn't a sound, either from the casa, or from the shed, or from the dormitory, or, it seems to him, from the whole of Vitry.

So he cries out.

Suddenly, terror. And Ernesto, without realizing it, cries out.

Jeanne comes running, rushes over to Ernesto, she's afraid. She asks Ernesto what's the matter. At first he doesn't know. Then he says:

I thought you'd all been dead for a thousand years.

The brothers and sisters heard him shout. They all come running from the shed. They've had a fright too.

I'm afraid of the chairs, says Ernesto.

He weeps. The brothers and sisters know Ernesto is a bit crazy. So they talk about something else. They explain that the father found the chairs among the garbage in the deserted shantytowns between the river and the highway. He wanted to give them to the mother so he and she could sit in the yard on summer evenings, but the mother wouldn't have them. So they both went off in a rage to the town center.

The older brothers said they'd put the chairs in the shed so they could use them themselves, and the teacher as well, and Jeanne, and you too, Ernesto.

Ernesto said the chairs must have been stolen a long time ago and then thrown away, and then stolen again and so on, and it was a good idea for them to keep them with them in the shed.

Jeanne sat down like a lady in one of the chairs, and two of the smaller brothers and sisters sat in the other. They were very glad to have them.

The kitchen door is shut. The kitchen is empty.

Ernesto knows the mother has shut herself up in the bedroom. He speaks to her.

Ernesto: What's the matter?

The mother's voice is slow, drowsy.

Mother: Nothing ... I'm just a bit tired.

Ernesto: You're in the dark ...

Mother: I prefer it ... Sometimes I prefer it ...

Long silence.

Mother: Have you just got back from Paris, Ernesto?

Ernesto: Yes. (Pause.) Where's Father?

Mother: At the highway, he went to have a look.

Silence.

Mother: How far have you got, Ernesto?

Ernesto hesitates, then speaks.

Ernesto, laughing: Various places ... I've done ... a

little bit of philosophy . . . a little bit of mathematics . . .
a little bit of this . . . a little bit of that . . .

Mother: What about chemistry? You haven't given
it up?

Ernesto: No. It's just finished, that's all.

Mother: Chemistry is the future, isn't it?

Ernesto: No.

Mother: No. (Pause.) What *is* the future?

Ernesto: Tomorrow.

Silence. There's a tinge of uneasiness in Ernesto's
voice.

Ernesto: Mama . . . what's the matter?

Mother: Nothing. I'm thinking . . . a bit about this, a bit
about that . . . like you . . .

Ernesto: It's as if I could see you . . . You're looking at
your hands . . .

Mother: That's right . . . I often look at my hands in the
evening . . . I like the time just before it gets dark . . .

Silence.

Ernesto: You get some peace and quiet then.

Mother: Yes . . . I think about myself, but not in an
everyday way—in general. (Silence.) Ernesto, I learned
a lot from what you were saying the other evening, about
there not being any point . . . It did me a lot of good . . .
the desolation is easier . . . and it's as if the loneliness
were more natural . . .

Silence.

The mother comes out of the bedroom. She sits by
Ernesto. Looks at him.

Mother: Ernesto . . . I wanted to tell you . . . Sometimes I think I prefer you to the others, and that hurts me.

Ernesto, crying out: What are you saying?

Mother: Don't think about it, Ernesto, forget I said it.

Ernesto: You're just tired . . . It's nothing.

Mother: That's right . . . It's nothing. (Silence.) Ernesto . . . about this school business, Ernesto, it'll pursue you through the rest of your life . . . It's a bad mark on your file, leaving school.

Ernesto: No.

Mother: Don't you think so?

Ernesto: I'm sure of it. (Pause.) That's all over.

Mother: You can't be a plumber with what you know . . . It's impossible. (No answer.) What do you want to do, yourself?

Ernesto: Nothing.

Mother: You won't be able to keep it up, Ernesto, no one can.

Silence. Then the mother cries out.

Mother: Ernesto, swear to me that . . . that what you want isn't . . . swear to me, Ernesto . . .

Ernesto: I swear it, Mama . . . I don't want anything in particular . . . not even anything terrible . . . I want nothing. Nothing. You can understand that.

Silence.

Mother: You're lying, Ernesto.

Silence.

Ernesto: Yes. Except with Jeanne, I want nothing.

Mother: With her you want everything.

Ernesto doesn't answer.

Mother: With her you want to die.

Silence.

Mother: Don't answer if you don't feel like it, Ernesto.

Ernesto: One day, yes, we did want to.

Silence. Slowness.

Ernesto: And then one day we didn't want to any more.

Silence. The mother stops herself crying out, her hands are shaking.

Mother: What day was it when you did want to?

Ernesto doesn't look at her.

Ernesto: The day after . . . after you told about the train in Siberia with that passenger . . . it was the night after that . . .

The mother, under her breath, asks God to help her.

Mother: Go on talking, Ernesto . . .

Ernesto: She didn't object . . . we didn't think . . . But afterward all I wanted was Jeanne . . . and we didn't want to die any more.

The mother's still waiting, faint with fear.

Ernesto hesitates and then tells the truth.

Ernesto: I don't know about Jeanne . . . I didn't ask her. I think . . . it was the same for her as for me . . . but I'm not sure . . . it's difficult to tell with Jeanne.

Mother: It's impossible . . . you have to go carefully with Jeanne.

Ernesto: Yes.

The mother is trembling but not crying. There's pride as well as pain in her expression. Jeanne is her, the mother.

Ernesto: I shouldn't have told you . . .

Mother: No, you shouldn't. And I shouldn't have asked . . .

Silence.

Mother: Leave me now, Ernesto.

Ernesto: Yes.

But Ernesto stays. Waits. And the mother goes on.

Mother: Jeanne has always been trying to die . . . only when she was small we didn't know.

Ernesto: She doesn't know, it was I who thought of it. *She* doesn't know anything.

Mother: No. She knows.

Dusk over the hills of Vitry. What sounds like a conversation between the mother and Ernesto. Jeanne stands listening by the stairs outside the kitchen. Their voices reach out into the empty yard, plunge deep into the hills, go right through the heart.

Mother: Were you hopeful about your studies, Ernesto?

The mother's voice is very slow, and dreadfully gentle.

Ernesto: Very.

Ernesto's voice also seems slower, more somber.

The mother is silent.

Mother: But now, Ernesto, you're not hopeful any more?
Ernesto: No.
Silence.
Mother: You haven't any hope at all? Do you swear it, Ernesto? You haven't any more hope at all?
Ernesto hesitates, but finally yields.
Ernesto: None at all. I swear.

For Jeanne and Ernesto things, days, no longer have the same length, the same shape, the same meaning. The love of the brothers and sisters is less urgent. The love of the parents probably less frightening. The beloved hills of Vitry have receded from the present. They are becoming part of the lovers' past.

But Jeanne and Ernesto scarcely feel these changes. For them they are vague modifications never put into words, differences taken for granted, a shift so natural and logical it seems merely part of a general revolution.

Nothing is ever said about this shift, even between Jeanne and Ernesto. And perhaps nothing is ever said anywhere else either, even in the parents' bedroom, about what sometimes gleams in Jeanne's and Ernesto's bright eyes. In the evening, at dinner, in that other light, the green and yellow light of the mother's eyes, this growing happiness can be seen as a happy sorrow. Yes, but a vain one too, as if it were in the nature of this feeling to be inexpressible, to get no farther, to be suspended on the brink of the void.

Another evening. Those murmurs are the voices of Jeanne and Ernesto. They're coming from the corridor where they sleep.

Jeanne: We don't know God doesn't exist.

Their voices are soft and alike.

Ernesto: No. We just say so, but we don't know. And even *you* don't know the extent to which he doesn't exist.

Jeanne: You say he doesn't exist in the same way as you'd say he does exist.

Silence.

Ernesto: What did you say? You said it as if he did exist.

Jeanne: Yes.

Silence.

Ernesto: No.

Jeanne: You said God doesn't exist in the same way as you once said, God does exist.

Silence.

Jeanne: If it's possible that he doesn't exist, it's possible that he does exist.

Ernesto: No.

Jeanne: How could he both exist and not exist?

Summer Rain

Ernesto: As he does everywhere in the universe, as he does for you, as he does for me. It's not a question of more or less; or of as if he existed or as if he didn't exist. It's a question of no one knows what.

Silence.

Jeanne: What's the matter, Ernesto?

Ernesto: Fear. And it doesn't stay the same, it grows ... It's maddening ...

Jeanne: Painful ...

Ernesto: No.

Ernesto has put his hands on his sister's face.

Ernesto: Don't cry. Please don't cry.

Jeanne: All right.

Ernesto takes his hands away from Jeanne's face. He brings them back to his own.

Jeanne: We're not going to die together now, you and I.

Ernesto: No, not now. You knew.

Jeanne: Yes.

Ernesto: How did you know?

Jeanne: From the story about the king.

Silence. Jeanne and Ernesto say nothing. The house is silent. It's night now, but very light, it's summer, the beginning of summer nights.

Jeanne: When you go away, Ernesto, if I can't come with you I'd rather you died.

Ernesto: If you and I are separated it will be as if we're dead. The same.

Silence.

Jeanne: You are going away without me, Ernesto . . . say it.

Ernesto: Yes, I'm going away without you.
Silence.

Jeanne: You don't want to be happy, Ernesto.

Ernesto: No, I don't. That's it. (He cries out.) I don't want to.

Jeanne: We're the same, Ernesto.
Silence.

Jeanne: Maybe we're dead already, Ernesto?

Ernesto: Maybe it's happened already. Yes.
Silence.

Jeanne: Sing to me, Ernesto.

Ernesto, singing: Long have I loved you. Never shall I forget.

Jeanne: That part always makes me cry.

Ernesto has stopped singing. He murmurs: Never.

Jeanne: Say the words again instead of singing them.

Ernesto says the words again.

Long have I loved you, says Ernesto. Never shall I forget.

Jeanne: Again, Ernesto.

Ernesto says the words. Jeanne listens to every one.

Ernesto: On the highest branch a nightingale sang. Sing, nightingale, sing, if your heart is light.

Jeanne and Ernesto look at each other through their tears.

Ernesto draws Jeanne's face against his own. He says the words of the song through Jeanne's breath, Jeanne's tears: I walked to the clear fountain, the water was so clear I went in.

Through their mingled breath, their mingled tears, Ernesto speaks. Long have I loved you, says Ernesto.

A thousand years.

Was the king alive then? asks Jeanne.

Yes. He was alive, he was still in his youth, full of strength and faith.

Silence.

You said a thousand years, Ernesto.

Yes.

Ernesto is silent.

Then he sings again.

Ernesto has stopped singing. They stay for a long time with their faces touching, not stirring.

We're dead, says Ernesto.

Jeanne, dead as he is, doesn't answer.

Say the words again, says Jeanne.

Ernesto: Long have I loved you, never shall I forget. Never.

The reporter bursts into the house. The mother and the father are there. He says he's come to see Ernesto. And that he's from the *Fi-Fi littéraire.*

Will he be home soon? asks the reporter.

Should be, says the father.

Silence.

The reporter looks at these people, the father and the mother.

Reporter: Are you the parents?

Father: That's right, Monsieur.

The reporter bows.

Reporter: Glad to meet you . . . Might I ask where your son is?

Father: He's picking potatoes with his sister, Monsieur.

The reporter smiles politely. He's trying to find an excuse to start a conversation.

Reporter, brightly: I didn't know you *picked* potatoes . . .

Mother: . . . No . . . but when the field's been harrowed they come to the surface.

Oh, I see! says the reporter.

The mother and father begin to regard the reporter with suspicion.

Mother: You ever seen Ernesto, Monsieur?

Reporter: Never . . . Is he tremendous?

Mother: Tremendous.

Reporter: Twelve years old?

Mother, vague wave of the hand: Twelve . . . twenty-two, twenty-three, I should think. If you want to know what Ernesto thinks, ask him.

Reporter: Are you pulling my leg or what?

Father: If you ask me he's twelve, twenty-seven or twenty-eight . . . Do you get me, young man?

Mother: It's to do with something but we can't say what.

Father: That's right.

The father's very forceful today.

Father: What's more we don't need to be told what age our children have to be, Monsieur.

The reporter starts to take on their way of talking.

Reporter: 'Scuse me.

Mother: Think nothing of it.

Reporter: But it would help me in my work . . . if I could find out . . . just a bit more . . . If it's not too much trouble . . . Might I ask you what you do, Monsieur?

Father: I don't do anything, Monsieur. Disabled.

Reporter: Really. In what way, if I may make so bold, Monsieur?

Father: Handicap. I'm just telling you what *they* told me.

Reporter, lightly: Part of the brain that doesn't function properly, I expect . . .

Mother: I agree with you. Something broken down.

Reporter, to the mother: Very disagreeable for you, Madame.

Mother: No, I wouldn't say that . . . no. (Silence.) How about you, Monsieur?

Reporter: Me? Oh, nothing, Madame . . . thank you.

All three are silent. General blank.

Reporter: You could tell me something about your means of support.

Mother: We get pensions, allowances . . . bonuses too. Nothing out of the way, Monsieur, but we manage.

Silence.

129

The reporter starts to giggle.

Reporter: Productivity bonuses . . . do you get them too, Madame?

Mother: I'd have to check before I could tell you that . . . For producing what, Monsieur?

Reporter: I don't know . . . Children . . .

They all laugh.

Reporter: I've met your daughter, you know . . .

Father and Mother, together: Oh, so it was you . . . you were the joker . . .

Reporter: Yeah.

He takes a good look at the mother.

Reporter: She'll be as beautiful as you, Jeanne will . . . And that's saying something . . . My, what a looker that girl is . . .

Father: And clever as her mother, too . . .

Reporter, sighing: Ah well . . . (Pause.) Your son's case is fascinating the whole of France . . . did you know that? The teacher from Vitry has been talking about him everywhere. He's even sent in a special report to the Ministry of Education. He's telling his story all over the place . . . Using it to advance his own career, if you ask me . . .

Mother: What story? My son hasn't got a story.

Reporter: That phrase he uses, Madame. The whole of France wants to know what that famous phrase means. That's why I'm here, Madame—to try to solve the mystery.

Mother: I understand it sometimes. And then it goes.

All of a sudden I don't understand it any more. Not in the least . . .

Father: It's true. She does understand the phrase every now and again.

Mother: Sometimes it strikes me as very distinguished, and sometimes it strikes me as a washout. So now you know.

The reporter waits for some explanation that isn't forthcoming.

Then he suddenly explodes with satisfaction.

Reporter: I just wanted to ask you when . . . when you realized your son's personality was out of the ordinary?

Silence.

The parents look at each other, surprised at the reporter's satisfaction.

Mother: I'd have to think, Monsieur . . . I don't know.

Reporter: Was there ever any little thing that struck you, Madame . . . some tiny incident would be enough, a detail . . .

Father: Perhaps the scissors would do . . .

Mother: Oh yes . . . let me think . . .

The mother suddenly remembers.

Mother: Yes, that's right, one day, three years ago, he comes in crying and shouting I can't find my scissors . . . I say, Just try to think where you put them. He shouts, I can't think, I can't think. Then I say, Well I never, and why not? And that's when he says it: I can't think because if I do I believe I chucked them out of the window.

Silence. General blank.

Reporter: 'Scuse me, Madame, but . . . even if you your-self were awfully intelligent, how would you have been able to tell from that that your son was a genius?

Silence.

Mother: There now . . . All of a sudden I can't under-stand what you're saying, Monsieur. It's too much of a strain.

Sigh from the reporter. Silence. Reflection. Then the reporter speaks. The manner he's caught from the parents is more marked than before.

Reporter: What I mean to say is, Madame, this story about the scissors, it hasn't got anything to do with the other one, the story about casting doubt on knowledge in general . . .

Father: Mind what you say, Monsieur. We're not com-pletely devoid of intelligence, my wife and I.

Reporter: 'Scuse me, Madame, Monsieur, what I mean is, supposing she weren't, intelligent I mean, she'd have been just as amazed by anything like that, like the story about the scissors, so long as it was about her son.

Silence, then the mother speaks.

Mother: Monsieur, that's not the way to approach it. I thought you'd understood what it was all about. Listen: that phrase Ernesto used—no one can understand it, no one. Except me. And that's because I can't explain it.

Silence. General blank. The reporter is depressed again.

Reporter: People have talked about the porosity of the

universe in connection with your son ... They said the universe was porous and knowledge, even if it wasn't taught, was in a way secreted by the universe itself ... So school was much less important than we used to think ... Have you any views?

Father: No. But what a pain that sort of lingo is, Monsieur.

Mother: Me neither ... If that's any help to you, Monsieur.

Reporter: But that phrase ...

Father, obstinately: What phrase?

Mother, obstinately: What phrase, for goodness' sake?

Father: Listen, Monsieur ... Just cast your eyes on what goes on ... Look at shipwrecks ... Nowadays survivors manage to hold out for six weeks without food or water ... in the middle of the ocean ... drinking seawater ... For two thousand years everyone said it was impossible, and now lo and behold they've tried and it *is* possible ... It's the same with our son's phrase ... maybe one day it'll have a lot of meaning ...

Reporter, beside himself: Hell, here we go again ...

Mother: Here who goes again, Monsieur? If you're not satisfied, Monsieur, why don't you just go home and go to bed?

Silence. Another general blank.

Then the mother looks out of the window and announces that Ernesto and Jeanne are back.

Mother: Look, here come our beloved children.

Ernesto and Jeanne come into the kitchen.

Ernesto is carrying a small sack of potatoes that he puts down on the table. Jeanne isn't carrying anything. They smile at each other, the reporter and Jeanne.

The reporter is taken aback by how big Ernesto is.

Reporter: My word, twelve years old . . .

Mother: Yeah . . .

The reporter greets Jeanne and Ernesto. He's had about enough of the parents.

Reporter, in a whisper to Ernesto, taking his arm: Could I be alone with you, Monsieur Ernesto?—It wouldn't take long, less than an hour.

Ernesto: I'd rather they stayed.

Reporter: Just as you like, Monsieur, I only thought . . .

Ernesto: It's about the phrase, I suppose.

Reporter: Yes.

Ernesto smiles.

Ernesto: Listen, if anyone can understand it it's them, our parents. They understand it so well they can't say a word about it.

Silence.

Reporter: How about you, Monsieur Ernesto?

Ernesto: Me? I think I did understand it once . . . when I said it.

Silence.

Ernesto: But now ... maybe I don't understand it any more.

Silence.

Reporter: It can happen.

Ernesto: So it seems ...

Silence.

Reporter: Yes ... Where have you got to with your studies, Monsieur Ernesto?

Ernesto: They'll soon be finished, Monsieur.

The reporter is very excited.

Reporter, babbling: Oh, excuse me, Monsieur Ernesto ... I didn't know ... When do you think they *will* be finished?

Ernesto: In a few more weeks perhaps.

Silence.

Reporter: The whole lot.

Ernesto, smiling: Yes.

Reporter: But ... you ... Monsieur Ernesto ... what about you?

Ernesto: About me? Nothing.

The reporter falls silent. Ernesto's sincerity has taken his breath away. He stops using the parents' accent.

Reporter: The frontiers of science are pushed further every day, or so they say ...

Ernesto: No. They're fixed.

Reporter: Do you mean to say, Monsieur Ernesto ... that ... so long as man goes on looking for God the frontiers will never change?

Ernesto: Yes.

Reporter: So God is mankind's biggest problem?

Ernesto: Yes. Mankind's only thought is for that waste of thought . . . God.

Reporter: And mankind's biggest problem is no longer its own salvation? . . .

Ernesto: No, that's bunk. It never was mankind's biggest problem. For a long while they thought it was, but it never has been.

Silence.

Reporter: Talk to me some more, Monsieur Ernesto.

Ernesto: What about, Monsieur?

Reporter: Anything you like, Monsieur Ernesto . . .

Silence. Then Ernesto speaks.

Ernesto: We're from Italy originally.

He stops. Silence.

Reporter: Do the other children do any studying?

Ernesto: No. None.

Reporter: None . . . Excuse me, Monsieur Ernesto, but how *is* it that . . . ?

Ernesto: It's very . . . I'm sorry, Monsieur, it's very hard to explain . . . What I *can* say is that we're all children, you see . . .

The reporter suddenly begins to understand.

Reporter: I'm beginning to glimpse . . . It's in the nature of things, if I've understood correctly . . .

Ernesto: That's right, Monsieur . . . In my mother's family there were eleven of them. In my father's family, nine. There are seven of us. Now I've told you the main thing.

Reporter: And so it was all for nothing . . .

Ernesto: No, there was no point . . . even less point than usual.

Reporter: Yes, I suppose you might say that . . . there was even less point than usual . . .

Ernesto: Yes.

Silence.

The reporter tries to prolong the conversation.

Reporter: Very high birthrate . . . in Italy . . .

Mother: *Very* high.

Reporter: Whereabouts in Italy are you from?

Father: Po valley.

Reporter, exclaims: Marvelous place!

Father: Yes. The Po valley mainly, that's us. We used to come for the grape harvest as early as Napoleon's time.

Ernesto is lost in his own thoughts again.

The teacher comes in. He doesn't go over to Ernesto. He joins the reporter. No one speaks.

During this long silence the mother starts to sing "La Neva," softly, wordlessly, as she does sometimes when she's alone; or when she's with Emilio, when they're both feeling a kind of unreasoning happiness and the long summer evenings have just returned.

The little brothers and sisters came to the casa as soon as they heard "La Neva" sung without words. They could always hear the mother singing it, even when she sang it softly.

At first they stayed out on the steps, then without making any noise they came into the kitchen. The two smallest sat at the mother's feet, the bigger ones on the benches by the teacher and the reporter. Whenever the mother sang "La Neva"—the Russian song about the river, from when she was young—the brothers and sisters came to the casa to listen. They knew she wouldn't drive them away, even if she was rolling drunk.

That evening as usual the brothers and sisters didn't know why the mother was singing. They knew something was going on, some sort of celebration perhaps, but they didn't know why.

That night, suddenly, the words of "La Neva" came back to the mother without her realizing it. At first it was just a word here and there, then they grew more frequent, and finally whole phrases came, linked up with one another. As if drunk, the mother was, that evening, perhaps from singing. The remembered words were not Russian but a mixture of a Caucasian and a Jewish dialect, with a sweetness dating from before the wars, the charnel-houses, and the mountains of dead.

Summer Rain

It was when the mother sang more softly that Ernesto spoke of the king of Israel.

We are heroes, said the king.
All men are heroes.

This is the son of David, king of Jerusalem, says Ernesto. The one who spoke of chasing the wind and the Vanity of Vanities.
Ernesto hesitates, then brings it out: our king.

Ernesto has cradled Jeanne's head on his arm, and Jeanne has shut her eyes.

For some time Ernesto looks at Jeanne and is silent, while the mother is singing again softly, singing again without words.

The king, says Ernesto, thought that it was in knowledge that he would discover the flaw in life. The chink.
The gate through which to escape from stifling sorrow, the outside.
But no.

The mother's singing has suddenly grown very loud.

Ernesto has lain down beside Jeanne.
Jeanne and Ernesto look at the mother and listen to her, wonderfully happy.

Then the singing grows quieter and Ernesto speaks of the king of Israel.

I, son of David, king of Jerusalem, lost hope, recites Ernesto, and I grieved over all I had hoped for. Evil. Doubt. Uncertainty, and the certainty that went before it.

Plagues. I grieved over plagues.

The barren search for God.

Hunger. Poverty and hunger.

Wars. I grieved over wars.

The ceremonial of life.

All the mistakes.

I grieved over lying and evil and doubt.

Poems and songs.

I grieved over silence.

Lust too. And murder.

Ernest stops. The mother's singing starts up again. Ernesto listens. But he also starts to remember the days of the kings of Israel again. It's to Jeanne he speaks, in almost a whisper.

He grieved over thought, says Ernesto. And even over searching, no matter how vain and barren.

And the wind.

Ernesto speaks slowly, with difficulty. It's as if he were entering upon one of those states known only to Jeanne and the mother, the smiling somnolence so near to happiness it is frightening.

He grieved over night, Ernesto went on.
And death.
And dogs.

The mother looks at them, Jeanne and him. "La Neva," at once fragile and strong, and of a terrible sweetness, goes on issuing from her own body.

Terrifying are Jeanne's and Ernesto's lives now, exposed to the mother's gaze.

Childhood, says Ernesto, he grieved over that very much indeed.
Ernesto starts to laugh and blow kisses at the brothers and sisters.

"La Neva" still.
A growing darkness invades the casa. It is night.

Love, says Ernesto, he grieved for that.
Love, says Ernesto again, he grieved for that beyond his own life, his own strength.
Love for her.

Silence. Jeanne and Ernesto have closed their eyes.

Stormy skies, says Ernesto. He grieved for them.
Summer rain.
Childhood.

"La Neva" goes on, faint, slow, mingled with tears.

Until life's end, says Ernesto, love for her.

Ernesto shuts his eyes. The mother's singing gets louder.
Ernesto is silent. Giving way to "La Neva."

Not knowing whom to insult or to kill, while at the same time he knew there should have been insulting and killing, says Ernesto.

And then one day, says Ernesto, he felt a longing to live a life of stone.
Of death and stone.

Silence.

And one day, says Ernesto finally, he didn't grieve.
Didn't grieve over anything any more.

Ernesto is silent.
Jeanne comes over to Ernesto and puts her arms around him. She kisses his eyes and his mouth, then stretches her body out beside the wall and so beside him.

It was during that night, during the mother's long "Neva" mingled with tears, that the first summer rain fell upon Vitry. It fell on all the town center, the river and the wrecked highway; on the tree, the children's paths and slopes, and the awful apocalyptic chairs. Fell thick and fast like a flood of tears.

According to some people Ernesto didn't die. He became a brilliant young professor of mathematics and then a scientist. First he was offered a job in America, then others all over the world, wherever there was a big scientific center.

So it would seem that because of this apparently placid choice, of what might be called a noncommittal kind of research, he eventually found life more bearable.

Jeanne's supposed to have gone away for ever too, the year after her brother made his decision. It's assumed this departure had something to do with the departure through death to which they both pledged themselves when they were little more than children. And that it was because of this pledge that they never went back to

France and the blank suburban place where they were born.

It's thought the father and mother let themselves die after Jeanne and Ernesto went away.

The teacher's supposed to have left Vitry-sur-Seine after the brothers and sisters were sent to an orphanage in the south of France.

Official sources reveal that he asked to be transferred to the school the brothers and sisters attended. And before he left Vitry he asked the court there to appoint him their guardian. The court ruled in his favor.

In 1984 I made a film called Les Enfants *(The Children) thanks to a personal subsidy from the Minister of Culture, Jack Lang.*

Les Enfants *was made in collaboration with Jean Mascolo and Jean-Marc Turine. The casting was also done collectively, by all of us. The actors were Tatiana Moukhine, Daniel Gélin, Martine Chevallier, Axel Bogousslavsky, Pierre Arditi, and André Dussolier. Bruno Nuytten and his team were in charge of photography.*

For some years it seemed to me the film was the only way of telling the story. But I often thought of those folks, those people I had abandoned. And one day I wrote something about them in relation to the locations we'd used in Vitry. For several months the resulting book was called "Stormy Skies, Summer Rain." I kept the last part, the rain.

While I was writing the book I went to Vitry about fifteen times. I almost always got lost. Vitry is a terrifying suburb, hard to locate and ill-defined, but I started to get fond of it. It's the least literary place imaginable, the least definite. So I invented it. But I kept the names of the composers, for the streets. I also kept the tentacle-like nature of this huge suburban town of several million inhabitants—I couldn't have done that in the film. I kept the parents' casa too. It got burned down. The Vitry City Hall talked seriously about an accident. And I was forgetting: I kept the Seine—it's there all the time, splendid, along by the now bare quays. The scrub has been burned. The roads by the river are perfect; they've got three lanes. The immigrants who lived there have gone. The company headquarters are palaces now. The one belonging to Le Monde is too huge to have squeezed into Paris, it's bigger than Bofill's at Cergy-Pontoise. People are frightened at night because the quays are deserted. Another thing I was forgetting: the tree is still there. But you can't see all of it because there's a high reinforced-concrete wall around the garden now. I know—I ought to have gone to Vitry and stopped them putting up that wall. But no one told me they were doing it, so what could I do . . . Now all anyone can see of the tree is the top bit, so no one will ever look at it. But it seems to be well looked after. The branches have been propped up, and it's even taller than before and very strong. It's like a king of Israel.

Yet another thing: I didn't invent the children's names. Or the love story that runs right through the book.

Also: the port really is called the Port-à-l'Anglais. The N7 is the N7. And the school is called the Ecole Blaise Pascal.

I did invent the burned book.